Praise for
THE CAVERN

"This book was amazing! It captivated me from the very first page. It had all the suspense, mystery, and excitement I look for in a dystopian novel. The characters were very well written and extremely lovable! The world-building was on another level. I felt like I was right there in the story. I can't wait to read more by this author and am truly shocked that this was her first novel!"
—Desiree Lewis-Dahlke, paralegal

"*The Cavern* is a powerful and captivating read that will appeal to fans of dystopian fiction. With its engaging characters, atmospheric world-building, and a mystery that unravels piece by piece, *The Cavern* will stay with readers long after they've finished the last page."
—Kristine Plent, third-grade teacher

"*The Cavern* is a must-read for lovers of all fictional genres! Immersive and imaginative, Kelly Keevins fully places you in her world of love and mystery and celebrates the unique ability of the human race to survive despite all odds."
—Erin Vieira, program manager at Advanced Behavioral Care Services, New Jersey

"*The Cavern* is a riveting tale of survival, trust, and hope for the future of humanity. The atmospheric setting is vivid and immersive, making it easy to be transported into this futuristic world. The author seamlessly mixes innovative elements with real-world emotions and relatable characters, which makes you feel like you are living the journey alongside them. The dystopian world Kelly Keevins created makes this book a captivating read."

—Katrina Mackrides, author of *The Salty Swan*

"*The Cavern* is a cozy mystery wrapped in a postapocalyptic saga for survival. It's a fun ride through an unknown future that ultimately lands in a comforting, human place—hope and love."

—Steve Schafer, author of *eMortal* and *The Border*

"*The Cavern* had me hooked from the first page! A perfect blend of suspense, imagination, and heart—this fast-paced and immersive YA dystopian novel is perfect for readers who love well-crafted, gripping stories."

—Natacha Belair, award-winning author of *A Stellar Purpose* trilogy

"Set in a near-future timeline where the air has become toxic from biological warfare, Kelly Keevins' haunting debut follows a young woman, Elsie, as she awakens in an underground cavern with no memory of the preceding events. From the opening page, readers are drawn into the mystery of this story as Elsie tries to piece together what happened to her and regain her memories—all while attempting to survive with others in a harrowing dystopian setting. Yet there is hope in this tale, and the promise of a better world. With engaging characters, riveting plot twists, and poignant exchanges filled with love and beauty, Keevins delivers a fantastic debut novel that promises to keep readers hooked."

—Mark Sabbas, award-winning author of *The Monarchs*

"*The Cavern* is a fast, smooth read with an excellent premise and mystery. *The Cavern* is entertaining for the reader to come up with a million different whys and is satisfying enough with the real answers in the end. Looking forward to the next story Kelly Keevins releases!"

—Sonia Lepe, assistant/screenwriter

"*The Cavern* by Kelly Keevins blends suspense, emotion, and mystery. Set in a shadowy underground world, the story draws readers into a chilling exploration of fear, resilience, and the unknown. Keevins' writing is vivid and immersive. The characters are compelling, especially the protagonist whose emotional journey adds depth to the harrowing narrative. *The Cavern* is a standout read for fans of dystopian literature."

—Shari Nemeroff, physical therapy assistant

The Cavern
by Kelly Keevins

© Copyright 2025 Kelly Keevins

ISBN 979-8-88824-694-8

All rights reserved. No part of this publication may be reproduced, stored in a retrieval system, or transmitted in any form or by any means—electronic, mechanical, photocopy, recording, or any other—except for brief quotations in printed reviews, without the prior written permission of the author.

This is a work of fiction. All the characters in this book are fictitious, and any resemblance to actual persons, living or dead, is purely coincidental. The names, incidents, dialogue, and opinions expressed are products of the author's imagination and are not to be construed as real.

Edited by Hannah Woodlan
Cover design by Catherine Herold

Published by

◤ köehlerbooks™

3705 Shore Drive
Virginia Beach, VA 23455
800-435-4811
www.koehlerbooks.com

THE CAVERN

KELLY KEEVINS

VIRGINIA BEACH
CAPE CHARLES

To Timothy Keevins

for being my biggest cheerleader and supporter.

I love you!

PROLOGUE

ANGELO SEES HER first. She seems to glow, like a goddess revealing herself to her people. But what goddess wears black jeans and a plain maroon T-shirt, her long chestnut hair hanging freely behind her? What goddess creeps in and gawks, looking lost and confused?

Who is this woman? Why is she here? Angelo finally wakes from his trance and is about to approach her when Marjorie takes the lead. Marjorie, a sweet older woman in her fifties, is the motherly type, the sort everyone warms to immediately. She is the best person to greet this strange woman and find out how she came to be here.

No one new has entered this cavern in over five years—since the bombs went off and the world above became unlivable.

Society was in decline long before the environment followed suit. As the human race became more ignorant and docile, those who craved power and fame let loose with all their worst instincts. Between the muted micro nuclear bombs, biological weapons, and climate change, the world was decimated within years. Weather patterns completely changed. Rain rarely happened, and when it did it, the skies released nothing but a sprinkle. The air looked yellow. Those who didn't die from weaponized plagues suffocated.

If not for the foresight of a few brilliant scientists and the funding of wealthy celebrities and businesspeople, the human race would be extinct. They came together to create these underground caverns that would sustain life as they knew it. They installed electricity and air filters to circulate clean air and created underground gardens and lakes, as well as housing and means to keep some animals alive.

When the air quality deteriorated, the average citizen, caught unawares, desperately sought shelter. Some discovered the caves and followed the tunnels to this new world. After tense negotiations, the scientists and wealthy folks allowed dozens of refugees such as Angelo and his family—his brother, sister, and mother—to live and work for them in the caverns.

Each brought something to the table, whether it was the ability to work or talent with a craft. Agnes, his mother, sewed clothing from the grown cotton as their daily wear grew tattered and torn. This was her contribution before she took ill and died from lack of medical care. Now Angelo takes care of his siblings, Mira and Marco, vowing to keep them healthy and well.

Time doesn't matter here. They believe five years have passed, but what day or month or year, only Angelo has a guess. His estimate comes from the markings he makes on the walls in his cave, but he doesn't always remember to make them.

This is what life has become. There are about fifty people in their cavern. Each has a little nook carved out where they "room," but otherwise, when they are not working, they come together around the tables in the grand meeting room. It is here they read whatever books were saved, play whatever games have been preserved or created, and converse.

It is here that *she* appears, as though from the thin air circulating among these dwellings. And Angelo is determined to find out exactly where she materialized from.

CHAPTER ONE

ELSIE AWAKES ON the floor of a dark dirt tunnel. There is a large metal door behind her, sealed shut and barely lit by a distant light at the other end of the shaft. *How did I get here? Have I been kidnapped and thrown into a dungeon?* She looks down at her clothes, an Arizona State T-shirt and jeans. At least those are familiar.

The last thing she remembers is coming back from class to study for her business final, her last before graduation. She plans to intern at Marcel Institute for the summer. *Was I drugged? When would I have been drugged?* The only option she has is to go to the light. Always an ominous phrase. But she moves to the light.

When she follows the light to an opening in the side of the passage, she finds a large cavern filled with people. The tunnel continues into the distance.

The cavern walls are carved from sedimentary rock. Lines of red, orange, yellow, and brown circle what feels remarkably like a grand hall. It would be beautiful if it didn't freak her out. There are tables and chairs set up in the middle, and dozens of people are sitting around, either playing games or cards or reading books amid a murmur of conversation. Dark holes along the walls lead to other, smaller caves.

Elsie stares. *Is this some strange underground club?* Just as her panic begins to rise, she is approached by an older woman with kind eyes. If she isn't a grandma, she should be. Her hair is a mix of blond and white, and she's wearing a T-shirt with kittens on it and flower-printed white pants.

"Hello," the woman says gently. "Where did you come from, dear? My name is Marjorie."

She extends her hand, and Elsie takes it automatically, then keeps her hand in this woman's, drawing comfort from this sympathetic stranger.

"My name is Elsie. I don't know where I came from. I just woke up and there I was." She points to the opening. "I don't remember anything." Her eyes prickle with confused tears.

"Okay, Elsie. What is the last thing you remember? Did you come from another cave? Did you come from the elite side?" Marjorie's voice is concerned but calm.

"The last thing I remember is being in my dorm room," Elsie says. The woman's other questions don't make sense.

"Dorm room? Where, dear? Outside? That is not possible; you wouldn't be able to breathe," Marjorie insists.

Elsie inhales sharply. *What is this woman talking about?*

"What year do you think it is, dear?" Marjorie asks.

"It's 2035," Elsie states. Marjorie nods, not taking her eyes off Elsie. She points to a chair and implores Elsie to sit. Elsie refuses.

"Dear, I think you should sit down. This may be quite a shock to you." Marjorie motions with her hand. "Carlos, Angelo."

Two men step out from the small crowd that has gathered, one around the same age as Marjorie, the other slightly older than Elsie. Marjorie shares what Elsie said.

"Hello, my name is Angelo," the younger looking of the two greets her. He is handsome and carries an air of authority. "Marjorie tells us you have lost your memory. Do you remember anything about the bombings? Where have you been staying the past five years?"

Elsie loses her balance and almost falls over. Angelo catches her and guides her to the chair. That seems to get everyone's attention. Conversations cease, and all are now staring in Elsie's direction.

"Did you say five years?" Elsie is having trouble breathing, but it has nothing to do with the air quality.

"Here, dear, have some water. It is filtered and purified." Marjorie hands her a glass filled with slightly cloudy water. Elsie sips it hesitantly, not wanting to make herself sick.

Angelo asks again if she remembers how the world ended, watching her as if looking for a certain reaction or like she will suddenly recollect everything.

"I-I don't remember. The last thing I remember is getting ready for my exam. It was my last one. I'm graduating this year. I mean, I was going to graduate." Elsie trails off and gazes past the onlookers. "What happened to me? Why can't I remember anything? Is this a joke? A senior prank? Oh my God." Elsie presses the heel of her hand to her forehead.

Carlos says, "Sweetie, I can assure you this is not a joke. But you are in a safe place, and we can help you."

Angelo pulls Carlos and Marjorie aside. Elsie can barely hear what they're saying, but she manages to catch that Angelo isn't "buying" her "act." He also mentions something about "working for the elite." She feels like she might vomit.

"Angelo, don't be an ass." A young woman about Elsie's age pushes Angelo aside, then approaches Elsie serenely. She is as beautiful as Angelo is handsome, with the same tan skin and almond-shaped eyes, though hers are hazel to his brown. Her shoulder-length brown hair has a wave to it.

"My name is Mira. He's my brother." She points to Angelo, then flaps her hand toward a younger, softer version of Angelo with black hair. "This is Marco, my other brother. It's clear that no one knows how you got here or where you are from, but I am sure after some rest and food, you will start to remember. You can stay with us until we find out more information—"

"Have you lost your mind? We don't know where she's from or who she is!" Angelo shouts.

"My name is Elsie Fitzgerald." She looks Angelo right in the eyes. "I know who I am. I just can't remember anything else. And I don't know what you people are talking about."

"Elsie, I can talk you through what happened, and we can figure out where you came from," Mira says. "I am making it my personal mission to help you transition into now. Let's get you some food, and you can sleep."

Angelo takes Mira by the arm and pulls her to the side, but his voice carries clearly this time.

"She can sleep on the floor in your room. She is not taking your bed or anyone else's. This is not a wounded puppy, and you can't just trust someone you don't know."

He sidles closer to Marjorie and Carlos, and Elsie hears him mutter, "This way I can keep an eye on her." Marjorie and Carlos nod in agreement.

Mira rolls her eyes. "Come with me, Elsie, and I'll get you settled. Marco, please make her a plate of fruit and veggies so she can get something in her stomach."

"That isn't necessary. I don't want to waste food right now with how I'm feeling." Elsie puts a hand to her stomach. Mira gently takes it and leads the way to a side cave to the left of the opening from the tunnel. "The first year or so, we dug out from the cavern to create rooms for everyone," she explains as they walk. "You can stay with me. It's basically arranged like a suite with a little common area. I share this one with two more rooms carved out for Marco and Angelo. Angelo was a contractor before all this happened, so he helped everyone as much as he could."

The common area has a table, two chairs, and a small shelving system that holds food and metal bins. Starting from the left, the first smaller cave is furnished with a mattress, blankets, and a pillow. At the foot of the bed is a small bin with a book and lamp on the lid. The next room has the same setup. To the right is a smaller cave that holds an extra-large reclining chair, a small TV table, and another bin.

Mira nods toward the cave with the recliner. "Angelo's room. In front of us is Marcos, and mine is to the left here. We keep clothes and blankets and such in the bins. We'll see if we have an empty one for you." She ducks into her small nook. "I have some extra blankets that we can use to make a bed for you. Why don't we take turns with the mattress? You can have it for tonight. Sound fair?"

"Um, okay, sure. How did you guys get everything?"

"The Elite—that's what we call the people who created this place—gave us some oxygen tanks to scavenge the town back when we first got here." This time Elsie senses a capital "E" in "Elite" and wonders what kind of dystopian class system she's wandered into. "We grabbed what we could for us and for them. Eventually the oxygen ran out and we had to make do with what we got. That's why we made sure to grab not only essentials and food but also books and games and such. We knew we would be here for a while and wanted to make sure we had things to do." Mira pauses. "Do you really not remember anything?"

"Last I knew, I was in my dorm at Arizona State. I was studying for finals. I keep trying to think about what happened after that, and it's just cloudy. Literally cloudy. Almost like I'm going blind or something. Nothing else comes to my mind clearly. It is so frustrating!" Elsie groans as she flops on the mattress. "Can you please tell me what happened? Maybe that will spark something."

"Sure!" Mira perches next to Elsie. "First the countries started warring with each other," she begins matter-of-factly. "The US didn't get involved too much, but then Russia sent a micro nuclear bomb to the capital, and everything went to hell in a handbasket."

"A nuclear bomb?" Elsie gasps.

"A micro nuclear bomb. It packs a lighter punch and not as much radiation. But if you use enough of them, well, they might as well have used a couple regular ones!

"The US developed a drone system to detect micro bombs and blast them in the air. But everyone was sending them left and right to almost every country. That's why the air quality started to diminish. Then a bomb was sent to New York, and the drone didn't detect it. The city was obliterated. Soon after New York, bombs started hitting all the major cities—LA, Vegas, Philadelphia, Dallas—"

"My family is from Dallas! Did anyone survive?!" Elsie interrupts. They were all living there: her mother, father, brother, sister, grandparents, her friends—everyone.

Mira regards her sympathetically. "I am so sorry, Elsie. If there were any survivors, it was very few. And if they did survive the attack, I doubt they survived the particulates. It became unlivable. People were dying left and right. It's a miracle we survived, to be completely honest. I couldn't stop coughing for a few months after we moved down here."

Elsie tries to collect herself. Her whole family is gone. Tears fill her eyes. *How did I end up here after all of this? Where is here?* After a few minutes, she wipes her wet cheeks and looks at Mira, who seems unsure what to do. "How did you all end up here?" Elsie asks.

"We're from Santa Fe, but we fled after what happened to New York," Mira says. "Angelo had overheard some coworkers talking about side jobs working on tunnels in the mountains in Arizona, and he figured going underground was our best bet. So we went to the mountains and found these tunnels. Then we discovered this cavern, where a few other people had already congregated. Angelo went out with a few other guys to gather what people and supplies they could find and bring them down. They constructed a seal to block off the outside air. But we didn't know what would happen when we ran out of air altogether.

"Thankfully, a couple of weeks in, two strangers came in and asked how we got there. Apparently, some scientists and businessmen foresaw the world going to shit and prepared underground dwellings for them to live in, complete with air filters, electricity, gardens, a small farm, and even an underground lake that filters water for everyone to drink. I don't know how, but it does; I leave all that stuff to the scientists."

Mira smiles a little anxiously, no doubt worried about how well Elsie is taking all this. "We call them the Elite. It started out as a joke because their machines are all stamped 'AHLEET', but we never see them, so they do feel like distant lords. And they were all set to get their hands dirty to maintain these communities until they found us 'ordinary' people," Mira says with air quotes. "They told us that if we maintained this underground city, they would give us food rations and materials to make clothing and medical items and so on."

She cocks her head at Elsie. "How are you doing? Is this too much for you?"

Elsie sighs, "No. Well, the part about losing my family is devastating. Everything else is just, well, I don't know. Nothing rings a bell. I must have known that my family died. I can't imagine being alive and not knowing that. Do you think I am an Elite and I fell and hit my head or something?"

"That's what I would like to know." Angelo enters the suite and glares into Mira's room with his arms crossed. "Still no memory?"

"Angelo, she has just had a devastating blow and doesn't need the third degree from you. Shoo." Mira waves her arms at him. "Besides, I would think this faded T-shirt and jeans would be, no offense, too dingy for them."

"Unless that's the plan." Angelo narrows his eyes. "Maybe she was sent here to make sure we're using our rations wisely and not making plans to overtake them."

"Why would you be plotting to overtake the people who enable you to exist?" Elsie asks with a frown.

"We are not," he snaps. "Leave us alone and let us continue to do what we are doing."

"Do you hear how ridiculous you sound? This poor girl lost her memory, her family, and who knows what else in the matter of an hour, and you are berating her? Seriously, Angelo, get out. Let her rest and absorb the information she has been given. Tomorrow, Elsie, I'll show you where we work, and we'll look for a good space to build you your own room."

Mira shoves Angelo out of the space and exits behind him, leaving Elsie alone with her thoughts and her sorrow.

How could I forget all that has happened? She can understand why she would want to forget. But why now? Where has she been for the last four or five years? *Did something traumatic happen?*

Her head feels like it may explode. Closing her eyes, she lies back on the mattress, rolls over, and begins to cry.

CHAPTER TWO

MIRA STANDS BACK with Marco while Angelo, Carlos, and Marjorie discuss their new arrival.

"I just don't trust her. How did she arrive here all of a sudden? Maybe the Elite sent her to make sure we're staying in line."

"Are we out of line?" Mira interrupts, unable to keep quiet. "If she is a spy, who cares? We aren't planning a mutiny. That being said, she looked terrified and then destroyed when she heard about Dallas and her family. I don't think you can fake that kind of emotion."

"An actress can," Marco offers. "I don't think she's a spy, but if she was, she would be an actress."

"She looked genuinely distressed, Angelo," Marjorie agrees with Mira. "I know you think I'm a softie, but I believe her."

"I agree with Angelo," Carlos interjects. "She couldn't have come from the outside, so she must have come from the tunnels. For her to have no memory of the past five years is impossible. Since the moment the bombs hit? There is no way that just happens."

Carlos pauses then adds, "You were younger when the Elite first came around here to check on us. I have told the stories to Angelo, and he was aware of some of it. They used to watch us like hawks and inventory our rations. Maybe they fear we have become too complacent. Nothing else adds up."

"Maybe she was experimented on," Marco excitedly throws from left field. "Maybe she escaped, hit her head, and forgot what they did to her!" The group stares. "Okay, fine, if my opinion isn't valued here, I'll go hang out with Andrea." He sniffs and strides to the other side of the cavern.

"As preposterous as that sounds, he might not be wrong," Mira says. "She could have escaped the Elite. We don't know what she's been through, and neither does she." She meets Angelo's eyes as she says this, daring him to argue the point.

"Okay, we don't have enough information," Angelo concludes. "In the meantime, we will take turns keeping watch over her. Between the four of us, we will learn as much as we can. Mira, tomorrow morning, help her find a spot for a room and see if she needs to grab anything from our extra supplies in the back. I'll take her to the gardens in the afternoon. If we make it seem like we are trying to get her acclimated, she might either remember something or at the very least let her guard down. Does that sound like a good plan?" Angelo asks.

"Sounds good to me," Carlos says.

Mira nods.

"Me too," Marjorie says. "I'll make myself available before you take her to the gardens, Angelo, so she can look through the supplies."

"Thank you, everyone. Hopefully we will get to the bottom of this," Angelo says. "Be careful tonight, Mira. Make sure that she gets a restful sleep."

"I'll do my best to make sure she doesn't suffocate me while I'm sleeping," Mira teases her brother as she saunters off to the rooms.

Mira finds Elsie wrapped in blankets on the floor, staring at the ceiling. Her eyes look glazed over and puffy from crying.

Mira kneels beside her. "Are you okay, Elsie? You can take the mattress. It's fine with me."

"It felt weird. Like I'm a guest, which I know I am, but I . . . it was just weird. I'm trying to process all of this. It's just too much." Elsie rolls to her side away from Mira. Mira places a hand on her shoulder.

"Try to get some rest. We'll figure it out. In the meantime, we'll make sure you fit in here. I promise you will start to feel like one of us—part of our family."

"Thank you, Mira. I appreciate it."

* * *

Elsie is awake, sitting up, and rubbing her eyes when Mira rouses.

"Good morning, Elsie. How did you sleep?"

Elsie shrugs. "I slept. I dreamed I was walking in a field of purple flowers and started choking. Someone came up to me and kissed my forehead, and I stopped choking. We lay in the flowers for a while, but I never saw his face. I woke up and thought maybe I was still dreaming. That maybe this was all a part of the dream. I guess it isn't," she says, staring down at her hands.

Mira says, "Well, we can't spend the day wishing this were all a dream, though, trust me, I have—*many* times. Today we have a full schedule. I want to show you some potential spots where we can carve you out a room. Then Marjorie is going to look through clothing with you to find a couple outfits in your size. After that, Angelo wants to take you to the gardens to show you how we do our chores. I think that's enough, right?"

"Oh no, not Angelo. He hates me. Why would he want to take me to the gardens?" Elsie whines as she collapses onto her blanket bed. She finds it easier to focus on these quibbles than the fact that the world has ended. Keeping her view microscopic is the only way to keep her sanity at this point.

"Because it is important that you see how we do things here and earn our keep," Angelo states from the doorway. "The Elite built these caverns, and it is their right to kick us out to die, but they don't as long as we work the caverns and tunnels for them. It is our livelihood. We must see where you will be useful." He adds, "I don't hate you. I don't know you, so I don't trust you. I'm sure in time that will change so long as you are who you say you are."

Elsie sits up and glares at him. "Do you hover over everyone and listen to their conversations or just me?"

"It's an older-brother thing, Elsie. He does it to me all the time. I'm just glad I don't have a journal I need to hide from him," Mira quips, standing.

Angelo smiles seemingly in spite of himself. "I filled up two water basins for you both to clean up. I picked up an extra toothbrush for you, Elsie. I was amazed I even found one in the bathroom bin," he adds as he walks back to his room.

"Thank you, Angelo," Mira shouts after him. She turns to Elsie. "He takes some getting used to, but he really is a great guy. You'll see."

"I'll take your word for it. I just want to figure out what happened and where I came from. Maybe I can go back there." Elsie catches herself. "I'm sorry. You've been so welcoming. I'll do my best to learn how things work here and mesh."

"I get it! This is a truly odd situation. But you came from somewhere, and I'm sure we can sort it out. Meanwhile, let's get cleaned up." Mira guides her to the common area, where Angelo set up the wash bins. They hunch over the water to wash their faces and brush their teeth; then Elsie pops her head back up in surprise.

"These bins smell like roses. How is that possible?" she asks.

Mira smiles. "We find luxuries where we can. One of the water treatment people collects extracts from plants and adds it to our washing water. Some days it's citrus, some days peppermint. Most days it's rose, though. That's my favorite."

"That would be mine too. I love flowers."

Mira straightens and asks, "Are you ready to go find a room? The extra caves are just this way." She guides Elsie into the grand room, past the tables and the main tunnel entrance and toward the back of the cavern. They halt when three children dart out of a cave residence and almost run into Elsie. The trio, two boys and an older girl, appear to range in age from around five to ten years old.

"Oh, hi! Mommy, Mommy! The new girl is going to live by us!" the girl shouts in the direction they came from.

A woman maybe a few years older than Elsie emerges. She has beautiful dark skin and a mass of long, curly black hair. What Elsie notices most is the warmth and reassurance exuded by her dark eyes.

"Hello there. I'm Andrea. This rowdy crew belongs to me." She pats them each on the head when she says their name, from oldest to youngest. "This is Tabby, this is Elton, and this little character is Zander. Welcome to our cave."

"Thank you. I wish I could say it was a pleasure to be here, but since I'm clueless as to how I even got here . . ." Elsie trails off with a shrug.

Andrea blesses her with an understanding smile. "We heard all about you. It's hard to keep things quiet here. And there's no better place to find your footing than among us, Elsie." She nods toward her children, who are clearly getting restless. "I must get the children to the gardens, but if you need anything, please don't hesitate to come over. I'm right over there behind that burgundy curtain."

Elsie thanks her, and she leads the children to the tunnel entrance.

Turning to Mira, Elsie frowns. "Why is she taking the children to the gardens? Do they get to play in there?"

"No, children six and older have to work in the gardens. That's where they start to learn how everything works."

"Don't they go to school?" Elsie asks, appalled.

Mira lifts a shoulder in a half shrug. "We don't have anything formal. There are a couple of teachers here who work with them after chores sometimes. Marjorie, the woman you met when you got here, she's one of them. It's a shame, but we all must work and manage ourselves here. Their main schooling is learning how to work to survive."

"I guess that makes sense. How sad, though, that they don't get to be kids and play and learn like kids should."

"This is our life now. And after their chores, they do get to play. Marco adores them and plays with them all the time. We brought some balls and toys in from outside. Besides, there aren't so many of them. Andrea has her three, and there are five others." She turns and her face lights up. Marco is coming toward them, fruit gathered in his arms. "Hey, you just missed her. She went to the gardens with the kids."

"Oh man, seriously? I thought she was going to wait for me. I guess I misunderstood," Marco says.

"I think the kids were getting antsy, so she just went. I'm sure you can leave the fruit at her cave with a little love note," Mira teases.

"Shut up, Mira." He crouches to deliver the fruit to the family's stoop and then slinks off.

Elsie asks Mira, "What about the children's father?"

The other girl turns somber. "Andrea's husband died right before they found the cavern. Zander was just a baby when she came in with those three kids. They were so small, and she was all alone. Marco would visit and help her out with them. I am certain he's in love with her and she with him, but there is an age difference, and they're all weird now because of it. He was eighteen when they met, and it might be hard for her to look past that, you know?"

Elsie sighs. "God, I can't imagine how hard it's been for her—for everyone."

Surrounding Andrea's cave and three others that are likewise occupied, ten more hollows have been carved into the wall to mark where future home caves might go. There's not space for much more than that, and Elsie wonders how far into the future the cave citizens have looked. *Are they ready to be down here for decades?*

Shaking those doom-laden thoughts away, Elsie settles on an area two spots away from Andrea. Elsie can help her out with the children if needed but still keep her distance.

"We'll start digging it out tomorrow; you can make it as large as you would like, though if it gets too big, it'll get structurally complicated. But Angelo will make sure it won't collapse or anything," Mira says. "Let's get you over to Marjorie to get some clothes. I'm sure something will fit you."

"Lead the way." Elsie senses that Mira is keeping her busy so that she doesn't dwell on her thoughts. It isn't that easy, though. Losing her family and her memory remains foremost in her mind.

They reach the opposite corner of the cavern's rear, where a smaller room is carved out just deep enough to house storage bins. Each bin is a large heavy-duty black container with a yellow lid, and each bin has a label: Bathroom, Food, Children's Clothing, Adult Women's Clothing, Adult Men's Clothing, Medical, Tools, and so on. There are maybe thirty bins. Marjorie awaits them at the doorway.

"Hello, Mira, Elsie. How are you doing this morning, dear?" Marjorie asks, patting Elsie's arm.

"A little better. This is still so new to me, and I still can't remember anything. It's extremely frustrating," Elsie says, worrying that all she does is complain. Yes, her circumstances are awful, but these people are in the same boat and have been paddling it a lot longer.

"Well, hopefully we can find an outfit or two to make you feel more comfortable. That might help, if only a little. Have you girls had anything to eat today?"

"No, we washed up and headed here. I completely forgot to grab some fruit," Mira replies.

"No worries, dear." Marjorie grabs the bin labeled Food and

pulls it to her feet. Inside are bags containing what appear to be fruit bars. "Grab one or two of these, and I'll mark them off." She turns to Elsie. "Go ahead and take one. Jeremy, one of our citizens, was a baker. Each bar is wrapped and labeled with the fruit and the date it must be eaten by."

Elsie looks through the bin and grabs an apple fig bar. "Thank you."

Mira takes two. "I am off to the garden to harvest veggies. I'll see you later, Elsie!" and she runs off toward the tunnel entrance.

"Thank you for taking time to help me, Marjorie. You have all been very helpful. Well, for the most part."

Marjorie gives a small chuckle. "Don't be too cross with Angelo. He is our protector, and his suspicion comes from a good place." She pulls down two bins of women's clothing. "Let's look through these."

During their hunt for the perfect outfit, Marjorie shares that she was an elementary school teacher.

"Dominic, one of the other former teachers here, and I laugh about the good old days of teaching for the fun of it before it became a chore. Dominic taught history at a local middle school. I told him I didn't have the attention span to teach only one subject. I adored English and math, so I couldn't just choose." She winks at Elsie.

"Do you miss teaching now? Why don't you teach the children here?" Elsie asks.

Marjorie scoffs. "The last thing they want to do is sit with me for hours, learning about proper English, writing, and math. They work so hard in the gardens; they need a break when they get back. When we have a quiet day where most sit and read, I will sit with them and help with chapter books. But they get bored and then run off to play. We don't have the structure of a formal learning space, so it's harder to get them to learn. Tabby at least likes reading, so she and I will sit the longest and try to learn the words in the books. I like those times." She looks wistful.

Elsie values her education and is grateful she was basically done with it before all this happened. *Something should be worked out for the children of the cavern.* She doesn't dare say anything to Marjorie about it yet, but she decides to see what Andrea thinks about her children learning academic subjects.

After what must be an hour of sorting through clothes, trying a few on, and starting to feel human again, Elsie settles on a plain blue button-down shirt, a pair of blue jeans, a pair of black yoga pants, and a gray long-sleeve T-shirt that reads Keep Calm and Play On. She also finds three pairs of socks, flip-flops, and a pair of sneakers that miraculously fit her size-seven feet. Her current sneakers look much worse for wear, like she has walked miles in them, so she is happy to replace them.

"Thank you for your help. I'll drop these off in Mira's room so I can be ready for my next babysitter," Elsie chirps, trying not to sound bitter about having to tag along with someone who doesn't want her company because he doesn't trust her to be alone.

Marjorie rests her hand on Elsie's shoulder. "As far as I'm concerned, it doesn't matter how you got here or why; but you are here now, and it's important to see how we live. And remember what I said about Angelo. He just needs to get to know you. It will be fine."

* * *

Elsie gets turned around on her way back to Mira's room and feels silly about it. It is a vast cavern, but she's essentially walking a big circle, after all.

Just as she steels herself to start peeking into rooms, Angelo emerges from the siblings' residence. He really is very handsome. His dark-brown eyes would make any woman giddy. But this is Angelo. She dismisses his denial earlier that he hates her; he has made it clear what he thinks of her.

"Ready?" he demands.

"Let me put these in the room. I'll be out in a second." Elsie sets the clothes down on the blanket bed, takes a deep breath, and reemerges.

"Okay, let's go." At once Angelo heads toward the entrance to the tunnels. Elsie tries to keep up, biting her tongue to keep from asking him to slow down. All she's eaten is the apple bar, and she feels lightheaded. *Is it all this moving around or being with Angelo?* she wonders.

Angelo begins, "Okay, so, I will show you several different sections today and explain the jobs that go with them. The gardens are this way." He pauses. "If you are truly ignorant of what happens here, I guess you will be amazed."

"There it is again." Elsie shakes her head. "That passive aggressive tone. 'If you are truly ignorant . . .' I am, Angelo. I have no idea where I am, and everyone has told me multiple times what has happened, and I am still in shock. So, please, can you tone down the sarcasm or whatever it is you're trying to accomplish with those statements? I'm trying to take this all in without crying hysterically." Elsie stalks past him into the tunnel.

"Okay," he says as he catches up with her, sounding subdued. "It's this way." He turns right, toward the portion of the passage she has yet to investigate.

About a mile down, the tunnel opens up into another cavern. Elsie's eyes widen as she takes in the scene before her. It is essentially a massive underground greenhouse. Rows and rows of fruits and vegetables stretch below heating lamps hung from the ceiling, and irrigation pipes are set up to water it all. People scattered throughout look to be either gathering food or planting. A couple of men on a ladder are replacing a bulb. To the far left is an actual glass greenhouse.

"This is the main garden where we grow all our produce. The

greenhouse is for more tropical fruits and vegetables that need more intense heat and not as much water. We gather what vegetation is ready to be harvested and take it to the back room to prepare for distribution," Angelo explains.

"This is amazing. I have no words," Elsie says. She sees Andrea gathering corn with the children and putting it in baskets. "Oh, there's Andrea. I met her and the children earlier by her room."

"Andrea is an amazing person. What she's doing on her own with those children is quite a chore."

Elsie smiles. "It's my understanding that she doesn't do it completely on her own."

"Yes, well, we all help." Angelo is interrupted by a blond woman who smiles from ear to ear as she approaches him.

"Hello, Angelo. I just picked some pears. Would you like one?" she asks, flicking her gaze dismissively at Elsie.

"Hi, Amanda. This is Elsie. She just joined us yesterday," Angelo introduces them without answering Amanda's question.

"Yes, I heard. Welcome to our humble abode," Amanda says flatly, as though Elsie is an inconvenience.

"I'm showing her around so we can start her in the rotation in a week or so. Great job with the pears," he states with a slight stutter. "Let's move along, Elsie." He hastens away, leaving Amanda with a dumbfounded expression that Elsie can't help but note as she follows him.

"Is that your girlfriend?" Elsie asks, giving Angelo a side-glance.

"Amanda is closest to my age, which seems to be the main qualifier these days. But my responsibility is to the people of this cavern and my family. I don't have time for that sort of thing right now," he says as he stumps through the peach orchard.

"Everyone has time for that type of thing. You just have to find the right person to make it work with. Oh!" she cries, distracted. "You have ginger and ginseng! I use these in everything! Maybe I can ask that baker guy to put together some bars using these."

"You mean Jeremy? I'm sure he can whip something up." Angelo hurries her along. "Let's go; there's a lot more I need to show you."

As they pass the men on the ladder, one of them calls down to Angelo, "Hey, Angelo, who the heck is this? A new face? And a very pretty one at that."

"Alright, take it easy, Mike. This is Elsie. She is a member of our community and will start participating in our daily chores." Angelo gives Elsie a look she can't decipher, and she realizes the mystery of her appearance isn't to be discussed. "Elsie, this is Mike and Bart. They are the head electricians here. They stay near the Elite cavern, so you won't see them hanging around our part of the caverns."

"Well, that could change now," says Mike. "So, pretty lady, do you need any help illuminating your life? I'm sure I can help." He comes down the ladder and leans close. Elsie is immediately uneasy.

"No, I think I'm good, thanks."

"Enough of that, Mikey. Does that line honestly work?" Angelo jests.

"Where does the electricity even come from?" Elsie asks, directing her question to Angelo.

Bart comes from around the ladder where he was spotting Mike, frowning at her. "The generators we connected to the main transformers in town. You don't know that already?"

"She's a bit sheltered. We had her working in the main cavern," Angelo answers for her.

"I thought everyone was working in this part of the cavern. I've popped over to your side before to fix some electrical issues, and I'm sure I would remember a beautiful face like yours," Mike presses.

"Well, I don't remember yours, and I am sure there is a reason for that," Elsie retorts.

Angelo laughs. "She's got your number already, Mike." He takes her hand and leads her toward the entrance across the way.

Elsie tries not to make any eye contact with anyone as she walks. She wonders if there is a terrible reason she escaped wherever she came from. At first she hoped someone would recognize her, but after her interaction with Mike, she wants to crawl into a cave and stay forgotten.

But gradually she becomes aware of her hand in Angelo's. She grows warm all over and feels safe and secure, which surprises her. She looks up to find his eyes on her.

"Don't worry about those guys. I've never seen them outside of this area, but if they bother you, you let me know." Angelo offers a small smile. For the first time, Elsie doesn't feel on edge around him.

As they enter the next cavern, Angelo releases her hand and steps inside. Before them is a series of tables with sinks. People are washing and shucking corn, peas, and other vegetables.

"Here we clean the fruits and vegetables and move them to the far corner to be sorted out for rations. Food is rationed at the beginning of each week," Angelo explains.

"This is amazing," Elsie gasps. "Where does the water come from? How do you get this much?"

"We recycle it, but it initially comes from whatever rainwater we get. It's filtered in the water processing room. Here, I'll show you."

Angelo leads her to another opening and down a tunnel about a half mile from where they were. The passage opens up into a huge underground lake complete with a milling wheel. Elsie finds herself continuously amazed at the scale of it all.

"See, the water is deposited in the lake from barrels that are collected from our washing bins and the sinks you saw in the other room, as well as drainage from the gardens. The waterwheel turns it, and it filters through those pipes back into the sinks you saw in the other room. We get all our water from those sinks. The Elite have a plumber that maintains the pipes with help from other handyman types who ended up down here.'

Elsie shakes her head. "That reminds me: Mira said something about an air-purifying system?"

Angelo points to the ceiling. "In this room, air and water come through those vents, which hold filters to purify the air. In the other caverns, you will see similar vents."

"The Elite sure thought of everything, didn't they?"

"That's why we are indebted to them. It took time, knowledge, and money to ensure that human life survives." Angelo turns very serious. "Let's finish the tour so we can get back."

"Okay." Elsie doesn't know what just happened, but Angelo has reverted to the surly manner he started out with.

Before they leave the room, Elsie notices another opening in the far corner. Angelo reenters the tunnel before she can ask about it.

Angelo takes her back through the cleaning room and through a different entrance. There, a short tunnel leads to a malodorous area. Large metal vats with mechanical arms are sifting soil and something with a terrible smell.

"Wear this." Angelo hands Elsie a clothespin and takes another from a line of pins hanging on a thread against the wall. He pinches the pin over his nose. "This is the fertilization room. We take the used soil and bring it here to be mixed with the animal waste. It is then brought to the garden for planting. Then, through here"—he leads her through another opening to the left—"are the animals."

Elsie is awestruck once again. In this cavern is an entire barnyard. Cows, chickens, horses, pigs, sheep, and many more animals are kept in different pens. A small, makeshift pasture past the pens and toward the back of the cavern provides an area to graze and expel waste.

"So, everything we ration isn't just for ourselves; it is also for the animals. We get eggs and milk, and when the animals get old, they are slaughtered for meat, but of course they are bred first. It is quite an operation. Sometimes it works and sometimes it doesn't. We lost some animals the first couple of years, but we did our best to preserve what we could."

Andrea and her children enter with their noses still clothespinned. The children rush to the opposite side of the pasture, to a medium-size pen holding dogs. There aren't many breeds, and Elsie wonders what they're for. She doesn't remember seeing dogs in the main cavern. Perhaps these are working dogs.

"Sorry, Angelo, the kids finished up earlier than we expected, so I promised them they could see the dogs. Tabby, of course, wants to take one back with us. I figured this was the best compromise." Andrea shakes her head.

"We're just about done here anyway, and I have to get back to the main cavern," Angelo says. "Elsie, let's head on back."

"Can't I stay for a bit?" she asks.

"I'll bring her back with us," Andrea offers.

"That would be great. Thank you, Andrea. Uh, see you later, Elsie." Angelo quickly exits.

"Well, that was interesting," Andrea comments as they join the children beside the dog pen.

"What do you mean?" Elsie asks.

The other woman smiles. "He seemed flustered. I think you fluster him, Elsie."

Elsie quickly changes the subject. "I saw you with the children in the garden. Don't you wish they could go to school and learn English, math, and all the other stuff we learned in school?"

"You get right to the point, don't you?" Andrea laughs. "Well, yes, ideally I wish they could get schooling, but our civilization doesn't allow for that type of thing, does it? I work with them most days on their letters and numbers. Marjorie does some reading with them. Marco loves math, so he plays math games with them." She sighs, leaning over the fence to pet one of the dogs. "But honestly, who knows how long we'll be down here? Knowing how to survive is the best schooling they can get."

Elsie can only nod. She has no idea what it has been like to live this way day after day for years. She doesn't want to push it. Instead she wanders over to the horse stables. Andrea follows, always keeping an eye on the children.

"Have you ever seen the Elite? Do they ever visit with you guys?" Finding a piece of carrot just outside of a stall, Elsie gives it to the stall's horse occupant.

"Not often. They are so busy trying to save the world. They check in with our leaders—Carlos, Marjorie, and Angelo—from time to time to make sure everything is working well. The original maintenance crew they brought with them is our closest connection to them. Electricians, plumbers, farmers—they were smart and brought with them exactly who they needed to run the whole place, just not enough hands. So it works out for everyone," Andrea explains.

"What do you mean they're trying to save the world? I thought that work was done when they made these caves."

"The central group is a bunch of scientists and doctors, I believe. They want to make the outside world livable again—change the atmosphere, I suppose. That's my guess, anyway." She shifts her focus behind Elsie. "No, Tabby, put the puppy back in the pen."

Andrea reasons with Tabby as Elsie struggles to absorb everything around her and everything she has learned. Her head aches.

"Alright, my brood, let's go back." Andrea waves at a farmer who has stopped by the dog pen with food, and the children shout goodbye to him and join their mother. The group heads back to their main cavern.

"I am just so bored, Mommy. And we would love that puppy so much!" Tabby insists.

"We don't have the resources in our room for a puppy. Farmer Dave will make sure they are well fed and safe here. You can visit again tomorrow, *if* you get all your chores done. We have a lot of planting to do tomorrow. I heard many seeds were collected today."

"I'm exhausted," Elsie interjects when they reach the grand meeting room. "I think I'll take a nap before looking over my new quarters."

"That sounds like a good idea. I'm sure Angelo will want to

check it out and make sure it's a good space to dig out. He's excellent at that type of thing."

"Oh no, not more time with Angelo. Is he like the president of the cavern?"

Andrea smiles. "He became one of our de facto leaders a couple of years ago. He just quietly shouldered the responsibility to make this place livable for us. Safe and easy. He really is a good guy."

"I wish everyone would stop telling me what a good guy he is. All he is to me is judgmental and rude."

"You'll learn in time that he really does have everyone's best interest at heart. If one thing goes wrong, this whole world of ours comes tumbling down. He would rather die than see that happen. He did get a little more focused and zealous after his mother died, but that's understandable."

"His mother died here?" Elsie asks.

"Yes. She used to take the cotton we grow here and make the most beautiful clothing. She taught a few of the girls here how to do it, but Lydia is the only one who stuck with it, and she doesn't feel confident enough to get fancy with it." Andrea's face brightens. "Angelo's mother made Zander a beautiful onesie. I was so sad when he outgrew it, but perhaps another child will get to wear it one day.

"Anyway, she got very ill, and the antibiotics we scavenged weren't working. She passed. We think it was an infection, or maybe even cancer. It broke Mira's heart. She was studying to be a nurse before all this and tried everything she could think of. They asked the Elite for help, but their doctors couldn't do anything aside from what we were already doing."

Andrea's voice sounds scratchy now. "She wasn't the first of us to perish, and she won't be the last. But that is what got Angelo so obsessed with making sure the rest of us are okay. He puts a lot on himself, so just go easy on him. I'll see you later."

Elsie is struggling to believe that the man hell-bent on proving she's a liar is the same man everyone speaks so highly of. She decides to give him a chance all the same, though she knows he isn't going to make it easy for her.

CHAPTER THREE

*E**LSIE IS IN a white room, seated on an examination table. There is a symbol on the doors: three arrows forming a triangle with a cross in the middle.*

"Where am I?" she asks calmly as a man in a white lab coat bearing the same symbol comes toward her. He wields a syringe.

"I promise you that you are safe. I just need some blood; is that all right?" he asks, inserting the needle before she can reply. The syringe fills with blood.

"Why do you need my blood? What is happening? Please . . ."

* * *

Elsie awakens with Mira shaking her shoulder.

"Elsie, Elsie, wake up. You're having a dream."

Embarrassed that she fell asleep on the bed, Elsie rolls to the edge and sits up, putting her hand to her forehead.

"It was so real. I was in a lab or something, and someone was trying to take my blood." She folds a knee up and rests her forehead on it. "I think I am crazy. Maybe I'm a mental patient and I escaped an institution and came here."

She looks up at Mira, who is clearly trying not to laugh.

"What I'm hearing is that you had a nightmare and now you think you're mental and maybe my brother is right."

Elsie lets out an involuntary laugh. "Okay, fine. I am a normal person in an abnormal situation for the sake of your brother not casting me out into some abandoned cavern."

Now both are laughing.

"Well, it won't be abandoned, but it will be your own cave, so let's go check it out. Angelo is going to meet us to make sure the area is stable." Together they journey toward the back of the cavern. Angelo is there already, measuring the hollow and poking a stick around it.

"Looking for bugs so we have a new protein source?" Elsie asks, trying to keep the atmosphere light.

"Very funny, though not a bad alternative. We tried it in the beginning, but everyone got thoroughly grossed out and started getting sick, so we decided to stick with beans and legumes." He turns and smiles just a smidge. "I'm making sure the surrounding earth isn't going to collapse in. I start with the outside and work my way in so I don't get trapped. Would you like to try?" He hands her the stick, and she accepts it with the gravity of a doctor accepting a scalpel.

"Sure." She sticks it up into the ceiling about one foot in from the opening. It's high, and she almost loses her balance, but she gets an inch of the stick in. Angelo catches her by the waist.

"Thanks." Elsie turns away quickly.

"The idea is to get the stick in just so much without any of the stones or dirt crumbling into your face. If that happens, we have to keep prodding to make sure it doesn't collapse, or . . ." He tilts his head.

"Or what?" Elsie asks, dreading the answer.

"We look for another cave, or you bunk with me for eternity."

Mira smiles brightly.

"Most likely the first option." Angelo gives Mira a warning look. "This seems good so far. Let's keep moving forward."

The cave goes about six feet deep and then stops. So far all their prodding has proven successful in that it did not collapse and they are not trapped.

"Okay, so this looks good. I'll talk to Marco and Carlos and see if they can start with you tomorrow in carving out this cave," Angelo says.

"*With* me? *I* have to carve out a cave?" Elsie almost shouts.

Mira laughs. "I said the same thing, Elsie. We all worked on our own rooms. It's only fair. It isn't as terrible as it seems, though. It shouldn't take more than a week or two. By that time, a new rotation will be arranged, and you'll start working in the tunnels."

"Does everyone work everywhere, or do we get assigned an area? I have some requests if we're assigned," Elsie says hopefully.

"Everyone works everywhere. Assignments rotate weekly, and we try to make the schedule a month in advance so everyone knows exactly where they will be. It's an easy process, and this way everyone knows everything." Angelo smiles. "Besides, if we went by requests, no one would work in the fertilizer room."

"I guess that makes sense. But please don't tell me you make the children work in the fertilizer room," Elsie pleads.

Mira assures her, "We aren't heartless. Past a certain age, the children work in every area except with the animals and the fertilizer room until they turn sixteen. We gradually work them into the rotation starting then. But enough of all this; let's get some food. I heard we're having scrambled eggs today, and I love eggs!"

The three of them move toward the tables where everyone converges after the chores for the day are done.

"The Elite workers, skilled laborers like the farmers and electricians, work through the night to make sure everything is up and running. They agreed to take night shifts if the leaders took the early hours. And that way we can eat, read, play games, and so on after work," Mira explains.

Wash bins set up before the tables allow everyone to cleanse their hands before eating. One long table holds all the food on it, and everyone lines up buffet style to get their meal.

"I hope you like eggs. Jeremy makes the *best* eggs!" With that, Mira piles her plate with scrambled eggs and runs ahead to secure seats with Andrea, the kids, and Marco.

"So, what do you think about our little paradise so far?" Angelo eyes Elsie with what she reads as suspicion.

"I am in awe of it all. But I wish you would stop looking at me like that." She scoops up a big spoonful of eggs and veggies each.

"I'm not trying to look at you like anything. I still can't wrap my head around any of this. Where have you been for the past five years? Surely you could not have survived in the outside world," Angelo confesses as he fills his own plate.

"I wish I had the answers for you. I promise I will tell you as soon as I do remember. Is that a deal?" She turns with her tray and offers Angelo her free hand for a handshake. He looks at her and merely smiles.

"We will see, Elsie; we will see." With that he turns and carries his food to a table with Amanda, Marjorie, and Carlos. Amanda spies Elsie and sighs, then makes a very showy display of sliding closer to Angelo and giggling. As Elsie passes them, she hears Amanda whisper, "That is awful you were stuck guarding that girl all day. Did you learn anything new about her?"

Elsie knows she can trust only Mira and possibly Andrea, so she will reserve her friendliness for them. Let Angelo and Amanda conspire against her. She has nothing to hide—or does she?

* * *

Elsie is sitting at a table in a white room. It looks like a cross between a classroom and an operating room.

She notices the symbol with the arrows and cross on the door. A woman enters and sits across from her. She is beautiful and familiar. Elsie recognizes her from a show she used to watch.

The woman leans over the table. "You are a very lucky lady," she says in a strong Australian accent. "It is fortunate our scavenger team found you when they did. How are you feeling now that you've had food and water?"

"I feel fine. Where am I? Am I in trouble?"

"Not at all. What is your name?"

"Elsie, Elsie Fitzgerald. Who are you?"

"My name is Lily. We have a lot of questions for you, Elsie, and we will help you, if you don't mind helping us."

* * *

Elsie opens her eyes, and Mira is gone. *It must be morning.* It's difficult to tell down here.

She forces herself out of the blankets and pulls on the new T-shirt, jeans, and sneakers she received yesterday. She is exhilarated that they are so comfortable; she can definitely work in this new outfit. Mira enters with a basket.

"Good, you're up and dressed! I can take your clothes if you like and wash them. I'm on laundry duty for me and the boys, so I don't mind doing your clothes as well."

"That would be wonderful. Thank you so much, Mira!" Elsie hands over her soiled clothing.

"The wash bin is full, so feel free to clean up. Today it smells like lemons. It reminds me too much of cleaning solution, but who am I to complain?" Mira shrugs with a grin. "Oh, and I left you an apple bar next to it. You'll need all the energy you can muster up for today," she adds.

"What are you up to this morning?" Elsie asks, folding up her blankets and stacking them on the mattress.

"I'm on seeding duty this week. I collect the seeds and prepare them to be planted at the end of the week. So exciting." She giggles.

"I better let you get to it. Where do I find tools?" Elsie asks.

"Don't worry about that; Angelo has it all covered. He and Marco went over there right after morning rounds and started. I told him I would send you over as soon as you were up," Mira informs her.

"I guess he can't wait to get me out of here," Elsie retorts.

The other girl sighs, and Elsie feels bad about harping on Angelo's behavior.

"It's just his way. Don't read into it. Well, I'm off. See you later." Mira bounces from the room.

Elsie is happy that her dreams last night were minimal. She only remembers being in the white room with the strange woman. She didn't feel scared this time, though. She felt like the woman was doing something positive, like curing cancer.

She sets off in the direction of her future room.

Just as Mira said, the brothers are there digging, as well as arguing about which direction to go.

"I'm telling you, straight through is best. That is the way we have all done it. She doesn't need multiple rooms the way we do, or Andrea," Angelo tells Marco.

"And I am saying it would be nice to do something a little different. Let's dig to the side so the room is more horizontal."

"Elsie. Good. I'm glad you're here," Angelo says, breaking off the disagreement when he spots her.

"That's something I never thought I would hear," Elsie jests.

He regards her solemnly as he poses their dilemma. "What direction would you like your space to go? Straight back or off to the side?"

"Hmm." Elsie thinks on this a bit. "Do I have an actual say in the design? I think we should go to the left a bit and then straight back. How does that sound?"

"Spoken like a politician. You like to make everyone happy, don't you?" Marco looks at her like he has her figured out.

She smirks. "I took a class on conflict resolution. Trying to find common ground where everyone gets a little of what they want seems to be the best option."

"Very well." Angelo hands her a shovel and pickax. "Let's get started on the best option, then."

The three of them begin to dig. They have gotten about another six feet in when Carlos enters. He tells Angelo he is needed regarding an argument in the garden room about the greenhouse temperature. Angelo leaves them to continue without him.

When Andrea shows up with fruit and asks Marco to take a break and walk with her, Elsie notices that Marco looks at Andrea in a strange way and remembers what Mira said about those two.

A little while after Angelo and Marco leave, Carlos steps back from hacking at the wall and wipes a hand across his brow. "I can't believe Angelo didn't grab a water barrel before diving in. We're going to need lots if we want to make headway without passing out." He points toward the tables. "I'm going to find us some water. I might need to refill the barrels from the filtration room, so sit tight for a bit."

Alone in the cave with her thoughts, Elsie grows claustrophobic. She decides to distract herself by visiting the tunnel and observing what everyone is doing in their respective areas. Whenever Angelo heads back toward her cave, she will return to it.

* * *

Marco walks quietly with Andrea at first. He wants to tell her he loves her, but he isn't sure how to begin.

"Tabby is getting better at soccer. I think she could've been a really good player if things hadn't changed the way they did," he says.

"I appreciate you teaching her. I know she won't ever be part of a team, but you are right. She has a natural talent. It's a shame."

"I want to talk to you, Andrea, about us," he finally gets out. He tries to take her hand, but she slips both of hers in her pockets.

"Marco, you are such a good friend to us. I appreciate everything you do for my children. They love you like a brother."

Like a brother, Marco repeats to himself. He did not expect that. He loves those children as if they were his own.

"The way you have helped us and the responsibilities you've taken on, I couldn't ask for a better mentor to them," Andrea continues.

"I love them very much," he says carefully. "I don't think of them as siblings."

"You should, though. I am much older than you, so it only makes sense. You are as much a part of our family as we feel a part of yours."

"Andrea, I'm trying to tell you something. I need to tell you something."

"Don't, Marco. It is a lovely walk, and I enjoy spending time with you, so let's not ruin it."

"It shouldn't ruin anything. I would think it would make it better," Marco says quietly.

"I remember the walks I took with Sergio. We would talk about work, what was going on in the world, and sometimes, we just walked in silence. Those were the best walks. We didn't need to talk about anything. Maybe we should try that this time; what do you think?"

She smiles over at him. Marco takes the hint a little resentfully.

It isn't time yet. One day it will be, though, and she will have to listen to him.

* * *

Elsie finds the water filtration room and enters it to check on Carlos. No one is there, but maybe that isn't odd. *Maybe he got distracted.* This seems like the perfect opportunity for Elsie to investigate the other opening.

Past the water filtration room, she finds a tunnel with real doors along each side. She meanders about halfway down and opens one on a whim. Behind it is a fabricated room with bedroom furniture, a far cry from the natural cave dwellings on the other side of the water room. Gathering her courage, she steps inside and inspects the photos and certificates hanging on the wall. The photos show a family—by the beach, at Christmas, children playing. The certificates are for a plumber. It strikes her that these must be the bedrooms of the Elite workers.

Alarmed, she backs out immediately. As she heads back for the opening she entered, she hears a voice behind her.

"Well, well, what brings you here? Elsie, was it?" It is Mike, the electrician from the garden. Elsie glances around to see if anyone else is around. Her heart jumps to her throat.

"Hello. I was looking for the garden and I got turned around."

"Well, that is a problem. No one is really allowed back here. I can help you find your way back." He moves in closer to Elsie. She feels sweat drip from her temples, and he wipes it away. She swallows in revulsion. "Why do you look so nervous? Is there something you're hiding?" His breath is hot on her face.

"I am not hiding anything, and I would like to leave now," Elsie states firmly.

"I just want to help. See, I heard people talking. I heard you showed up with no memory at all. I thought, *That doesn't sound right.* So I just want to help you. I want to help you remember how good it feels to be a pretty woman." He runs his fingers from her shoulder across her collarbone.

"That isn't a memory I need to remember. Please, just let me leave," Elsie pleads.

Mike grabs her by the arm. "Who are you, anyway? Where did you come from? If you would like, you can come live with me."

He goes to kiss her neck, and in a panic Elsie knees him in the groin. He doubles over and collapses to one knee. Elsie dashes through the water room, turns toward the garden, and runs right into Angelo and Marco.

"Elsie, what are you doing here?" Angelo asks as Mike hobbles through the doorway behind her. He sees Elsie and Angelo and beelines for them.

"This crazy bitch just attacked me," Mike groans. "I told her I wanted to help out with the cave, and she kneed me!"

"That's not what happened," Elsie whispers. Andrea appears behind the men. One look at Elsie's face, and she takes action.

"Elsie, you come with me. Let's pause the digging for today." She lightly touches Elsie's arm and guides her back to the main cavern and to Andrea's room.

"You don't have to talk about it, Elsie, but I am here for you if you do," Andrea says once they are safely ensconced. She has a small futon in her room with a chair next to it. Elsie assumes the small alcoves to the left and right with mattresses in them are where her children sleep.

"There's nothing to talk about. I wandered into the workers' quarters, I guess. It was a hallway with bedrooms, and Mike was there. I told him I got turned around. He touched me; I didn't like it, so I asked him to let me leave. He touched me again and kissed my neck, and I kneed him. That's all," Elsie said.

"Here, have some tea. Well, it's hot water and lemon. I call it tea to make me feel better," she chuckles. She pats Elsie's knee. "You did nothing wrong, Elsie. I hope you know that."

"Oh, I do. You think he's the first asshole to come on to me that way? I took self-defense so I would never find myself in any situation I couldn't get out of! I should've known assholes like that always manage to survive." The two of them share a knowing glance. Elsie is a bit shaken but feels much better with Andrea here.

"Excuse me, ladies." Angelo enters with a cursory knocking gesture. "Elsie, are you okay? I spoke with Mike. He said he was trying to help but you refused. When he came closer, you kneed him." Angelo looks at Andrea, who shakes her head. "He said he thinks you have a secret that he might have almost found out and that is why you kneed him." Angelo looks down. Elsie can tell he feels wrong about it even as he says it.

"And do you believe him, Angelo?" Andrea gives him a stern look.

"I have no reason to fight with Mike, but if he was improper with you, I will report him. I will inform the Elite if I need to." Angelo meets Elsie's eyes.

"Just let it go for today, Angelo. I don't think he'll try anything after this. If he does try me again, it will be much more than my knee hitting his groin. You can report something then." Elsie rises. "Thank you, Andrea. Thank you for listening and having my back." She turns and leaves without another word for Angelo.

Elsie just walks, wondering where to find solace. She thinks then of the barnyard. She's always felt comfortable around horses. They are so peaceful when calm, but startle them and they are a force to be reckoned with. She likes that about them.

When she reaches the farm, she finds it empty except for Farmer Dave, as Andrea calls him. He's well north of fifty with a full head of iron-gray hair and looks strong from working with animals.

"Hi there. My name is Elsie. I was hoping to take a break in here and visit with your horses for a bit. Is that okay?"

"Of course. The name is Dave. Have you worked with horses in the past?" he asks kindly.

"I used to ride them for fun every so often. I would love to learn how to care for them."

"Well, here you have to learn to care for all the animals, but for today, I would love to show you how to handle these beauties," he offers.

"I would love that too."

For the next hour or so, Dave teaches her how to move the hay, how to brush the horses, feed them properly, and how to speak with them.

"Unfortunately, we can't ride them. Too cramped in here. But hopefully, one day, these guys will see the light of day and feel the wind in their manes," Dave says with a misty longing in his eyes.

"Hopefully one day," Elsie agrees.

"Oh my God, there you are!" Mira storms over to Elsie and hugs her fiercely. "Andrea and Marco told me what happened. I can't believe that piece of shit came on to you! Sorry, Dave." She hugs Elsie again.

"Really, I'm fine. I just hope I don't have to see that Mike guy again soon."

"Mike?" Dave demands, suddenly much sterner-looking than Elsie would have thought possible. "What did Mike do now? That bastard is always up to something."

"He made an inappropriate pass at Elsie!" Mira informs him. "But our girl can take care of herself apparently and took care of him! I just wish I had seen it. That ass has come on to me so many times, and I just ignore him. I guess because I'm Angelo's sister, it never went past that. I am so mad right now!" Mira hollers.

"Okay, Mira, you're upsetting the animals. Elsie, are you okay now?" Dave asks her in a fatherly way.

"I am very okay now. Thank you, both of you. I am starving

though," Elsie admits.

"Good, I think pancakes are on the menu with fresh strawberries!"

Elsie smiles. "Breakfast for dinner happens a lot around here, huh?"

"It's quick and easy and accessible. So yes, it does." Mira laughs. "Let's eat and get back to the room. You have had quite a day."

CHAPTER FOUR

ANGELO BOLTS UPRIGHT on his massive recliner, his throat raw from calling out. He has the terrible feeling he knows exactly what he was yelling. Marco pops through the doorway.

"Is everything alright? I heard you shout," Marco asks worriedly.

"Shhh," Angelo hisses, hoping he didn't wake the girls. "Yes, I'm fine. I had a dream."

"Must have been some dream for you to scream Elsie's name in the middle of the night." Marco winks. "Don't worry. I won't tell anyone." He retreats to his room, and Angelo shakes his head, embarrassed. He doesn't remember much about the dream in the way of content, but he remembers feeling aroused and then terrified. He needs to find out more about this girl and where she came from.

Angelo knows Mike is a lying bastard, but he can't dispute that Elsie is hiding something. She knows something or has done something that she isn't telling everyone.

She did seem very disturbed after her encounter with Mike. He hopes Mike didn't do anything more to Elsie than she shared. Angelo has a good working relationship with him, but if Mike did touch Elsie . . . Well, Angelo can't think about that now. *If he comes near her again, I will deal with him.*

Angelo's watch alarm goes off. Time for the morning rounds. He doesn't have the luxury of working out his thoughts and feelings. He has responsibilities.

Rising, he changes out of his nightshirt and sweatpants and into his button-down gray shirt and jeans, then glances toward Mira's room before leaving for the water filtration room. Hopefully work will clear his head. After that he will continue digging away at Elsie's cave. The sooner she gets out of his space, the better.

* * *

Angelo is leaving the water room when he runs into Mike.

"Hey, Mike. You're up early today," Angelo greets him.

"I switched shifts with Bart after what happened. Have you seen that bitch today?" Mike retorts.

"Listen, whatever happened between you two, forget it. I'm not pressing you for information, and I am not pressing her either. Let's just say you two had a difference of opinion and stay away from each other," Angelo suggests.

"Bullshit. That little bitch is hiding something, and I'm going to find out what it is. You're telling me you've just accepted that she appeared out of thin air?"

Angelo lets slip his surprise that Mike knows the truth about Elsie.

"Yeah, I know. I asked around your cavern. I wanted answers, and she wouldn't give them up. When I wanted to further question her, she kneed me. That is suspicious enough in my book, and if you aren't going to interrogate her, then I will," Mike declares.

"Mike." Angelo smiles through his anger and steps closer. "You will stay away from her. If there are answers to discover, then I will be the one to find out what they are. You come near her again, and I promise you, you will be sorry."

"We'll see," Mike stomps toward the garden room. Angelo sighs and continues on to the grand cavern. He's surprised to find Carlos and Elsie there already, working.

"Good morning. How is it coming along?" Angelo asks as he grabs a shovel. He avoids Elsie's eyes—and lips, which he's pretty sure he kissed in his dream.

"It's coming along, I guess. About how deep should we go for it to be suitable?" Elsie asks.

"I would say a couple yards. It's up to you, though. How far back do you want it to go?" Carlos asks.

"I don't need much room. I know you all have work to do, so if you can just help me get a yard in, I can continue the rest of the way," Elsie says.

"This from the woman who was surprised to be doing it at all." Angelo marvels at the change in attitude.

"Well, it isn't as bad as I thought, and Mira is right. It is my room, and I should put the work into it. I guess when there's a goal in the end, I don't mind doing it." She sighs and rolls her head around her shoulders. "I just wish my shoulders weren't screaming at me."

Despite his logical mind screaming at him to get away from her Angelo approaches Elsie and asks, "May I?" as he hovers his hands over her shoulders. She shrugs and whispers, "Sure."

He digs into her muscles with his fingers and thumbs, rotating his thumbs to loosen them up. "When you don't use particular muscles on a daily basis, they tend to lock up when you do use them. That is their defense. I used to unlock those muscles for Mira. It usually helped her," Angelo explains. He looks at Carlos, who chuckles and continues digging. Angelo stops and grabs his pickax. "Better, I hope?"

"Yes, they feel much better. Thank you." Elsie seems to avoid his gaze now as she gets back to work.

After a few hours, Carlos excuses himself to help Dave tend to the animals.

"I'm jealous. I liked being in the barn with the animals," Elsie comments to Angelo.

Soon Marco appears with a whistle.

"Wow, you guys got pretty far! I'm impressed. It took Mira like a week to get a foot done. All she did was complain and push dirt around."

"She wasn't that bad. Elsie doesn't want to go too far back, so we'll just keep digging until she says stop," Angelo says.

"Well, you don't have to keep going. I can do it. I feel bad asking you to help when you have other things to get to." Elsie grins at Marco. "Or other people."

Marco shakes his head with a rueful smile. "You haven't been here long enough to start making those jokes. You need to be here at least two weeks before you can join in."

"Who said I was joking? I know you both have people you like to visit with and help out. Look at Angelo. Poor Amanda must be walking in circles waiting for him to get done," Elsie teases.

"I don't think Amanda is who—" Marco begins.

"Look at that; it's time to eat. Marco, is there any fruit out? I am just starving!" Angelo swiftly makes for the tables.

* * *

"What was that about?" Elsie asks.

"Nothing. He's just having trouble sleeping these days. Let's get some fruit." Marco smiles and grabs Elsie's hand.

At the tables in the grand meeting room, Elsie notices a young woman seated at the edge with a needle and thread, looking frustrated.

"Hello, I'm Elsie. What's your name?"

"Oh, hello, Elsie. I'm Lydia." She straightens as Elsie sits next to her. "I heard you were at ASU before all this happened, right?" she asks, waving her hand vaguely. "I was accepted there and was supposed to start in the fall the year it all went, well, when the world went to hell. I was excited to check out the desert."

"I'm sorry you missed out. You would have loved it. What were you going for?" Elsie asks.

"I was undecided, though if I knew then what I know now, it would be fashion. I would have needed the help." She gestures toward her needle and thread.

"Yes, I was wondering what you were making," Elsie admits.

"I can only make T-shirts, blankets, and sheets at the moment. I was learning under Agnes, Mira's mother. I started with blankets and socks." Lydia sighs heavily. "I don't have the skill Agnes had, and I am struggling."

"Well, you might just need inspiration. Do you think you can make me a curtain for my room? In maroon and yellow—ASU colors?"

"Oh, sure! A curtain is just like a sheet, so it shouldn't be difficult."

"Maybe after the curtain, you can try a pair of pants? Just think of it like really long socks that don't have feet," Elsie suggests.

Lydia looks at her thoughtfully. "You know, you're right. I'll try it. Let me get started on your curtain. Maybe it will get my fingers moving so I can try the pants. Thank you, Elsie."

"No problem. I'll be in that cave in the back over there if you need me or want to talk."

Elsie grabs an apple on her way back to the cave and runs into Angelo.

"What was that about?" he asks.

"Nothing. I need a door. I thought she could make one for me," Elsie says.

Angelo frowns. "A door?"

"I noticed Andrea has a curtain for her door, so I thought Lydia could make one for me." Elsie shrugs and continues toward her cave.

Angelo follows.

"Andrea found that curtain years ago. She didn't ask anyone to make it. Lydia is working hard on other things. She shouldn't waste her time on a curtain."

"Well, I think a curtain could be a good distraction, and then she might be inspired to make other things. No harm in providing inspiration, is there?" Elsie asks as they reach the cave entrance.

"I'm just saying it may be more of a distraction than inspiration," Angelo argues.

"We will have to agree to disagree."

Elsie grabs her shovel and pointedly starts removing stones and dirt from where they have been digging. Angelo sighs and begins carving out more of the wall. They work in silence.

* * *

During dinner, Elsie sits with Andrea, the children, and Marco. Angelo stares at them as they talk and laugh.

"What are you looking at? Do you want to join the party? I'm sure they wouldn't mind." Mira leans into Angelo, lowering her voice so Amanda, sitting next to Angelo but distracted by Marjorie, can't hear her.

Angelo glares at her. "No, thank you. I'm just trying to figure out her deal. You know she asked Lydia to make her a door for her cave today?"

"Sounds like a good idea to me. Maybe Lydia can make more of them when she's done."

Angelo glowers, frustrated with the way everyone seems to take Elsie at face value. "We don't need doors, Mira. We need clothing."

"Lydia has been struggling ever since Mama died. Making doors might get her out of her funk. I think you are being too rigid."

"Look," Angelo interrupts, "now she's going up to Jeremy. Do you think she's going to request filet mignon for tomorrow? Ugh." He jumps to his feet and marches over to Elsie and Jeremy, plowing right into the conversation.

"Hi, Jeremy. The blueberry pancakes tonight were amazing. What are you two talking about?"

"The ginger and ginseng bars I mentioned to you in the garden. I wanted to see if Jeremy could make some," Elsie replies.

"Yes, we were brainstorming combinations. I think fig and honey will go very well with them. I'll mix some up later on tonight so they set for the morning," Jeremy adds.

"Well, you don't have to jump on it right away. I know you're very busy," Angelo interjects, seeing exasperation on the cook's face. But Jeremy's words tell a different story.

"It's not a problem at all, Angelo. I was getting bored of the apple, oats, and berries. This will be fun. Oh, tomorrow we have a special treat. Dave told me two more of the chickens are ready to meet their end, and he wants us to have them for dinner tomorrow. I was thinking of that with potatoes? What do you think?"

"That does sound like a treat, but why is it a treat? Do the chickens not meet their end often?" Elsie asks.

"The Elite get first dibs on the chickens that die," Jeremy explains. "If more than four die in a week, we usually get about two of them. Or if Dave wants to break the rules." Jeremy winks slyly.

"That's enough. I am sure Elsie doesn't want to be bored by all the details."

"I find life down here fascinating. I don't get bored at all. Thank you, Jeremy, for the wonderful dinners and for working on those bars. I can't wait to try them!" Elsie says. She makes to return to the table, with Angelo right at her elbow.

"Dave doesn't really break the rules. That isn't what Jeremy meant," he tries to explain.

"Angelo." She turns to him with a wry look. "Everyone just

wants to survive here and live the best life they can. If Dave sneaks a couple chickens over to us, I think it's wonderful. Why do you care?"

Angelo stutters, "Well, it's just that, well—"

Unfortunately, Elsie catches on. "Oh my God. You still think I'm a spy?" She storms off to rejoin Andrea and plops down at the table, looking frustrated. Andrea leans in, and it is obvious that Elsie is telling her what's wrong. Andrea looks over at Angelo and shakes her head at him with a rueful smirk.

Angelo returns to his table just as frustrated.

"You look stressed," Amanda simpers. "I was thinking we could go sit in the water room and watch the wheel and talk tonight. What do you think?" She looks expectant.

Angelo barely hears her. "Jeremy just outwardly admitted to Elsie that Dave sneaks us chickens. I tried to explain that he doesn't really sneak them to us, and she got mad at me for implying she could be a spy for the Elite. How can I not think that? Am I wrong?" he demands of the table.

Mira and Amanda answer simultaneously.

"Of course!" says Mira.

"No, not at all," says Amanda.

Angelo immediately fastens his glare on his sister. "Mira, how can you think I was wrong?"

"You fail to see the terrified look in her eyes every time we bring up her memory. She doesn't know what happened or how she came to be here, which scares the crap out of her, and you refuse to look at it that way. Maybe just get over yourself and look into her eyes. Maybe you can see what we see." Mira leaves the table to join Elsie and Andrea.

"I agree with you, Angelo. There is something off about her. Be careful, or you might get suckered into her game like everyone else here." Amanda puts her hand on Angelo's.

"Thank you, Amanda. I appreciate it." And with that, Angelo leaves the table to go to his room.

* * *

Elsie finds Angelo sitting in his oversize recliner with a book. He has a soft LED lamp on and his feet up. He places the book down when Elsie enters.

"What are you reading? Or are you afraid I might tell the Elite that you're going to use knowledge against them because you read too much?" Elsie smiles to take the edge off her question.

Angelo shows her the cover: *Harry Potter and the Chamber of Secrets*. "It's pretty good. I put off reading them when Marco was a kid. I guess now is as good a time as any."

"My favorite character was always Ron. I guess I felt bad for him," Elsie offers.

"I like Hermione. Strong females always impress me." Angelo sighs. "I guess we better get to sleep."

"Yeah, don't want to get too familiar with the spy. Never know what you could be letting her know by accident," she says with biting sarcasm.

"Elsie, you have to understand where I'm coming from. We've been here for five years, and no one has entered this cave other than the workers for the Elite. You come in, and I'm just supposed to think you wandered in from outside? Or that you found us by accident? It's impossible. No one can survive out in the world, and there is no way you just wandered in here. I have to be skeptical. I am sorry it upsets you, but I won't apologize for trying to make sure my family and the people of this cavern are safe."

Elsie crosses her arms. "What is the relationship between you all and the Elite that it makes you think they would send a spy?"

"That's just it. We don't have a relationship. They come down once in a blue moon to check in on us, but other than that, they keep to themselves. It's just a matter of time before what we have ends. It's too good to last. I suspect the Elite are looking for a reason to be rid of us."

"What good would that do them? Then they would have to work the caverns, and from what I gather, they're too good for that kind of labor." Elsie leans against the wall of Angelo's cave and is again struck by how handsome he is. *Untimely*, she chides herself.

"True, but they are elusive and mysterious. It is hard to determine where their heads are at. If they think we are more of a hindrance than essential, they could kick us out at any time. They created this world we live in. They have the rights to it more than anyone." Angelo stands and faces Elsie. "Any information they are given, they could use against us."

"Or the information could show how essential you all are to this system," she says matter-of-factly. "I doubt they would see you as a threat."

Angelo stares at her. "Do you see us as a threat?"

"No." Elsie breaks eye contact and looks at her feet. "Good night, Angelo."

That night, she can't sleep. She tosses and turns on her makeshift bed on the floor. The sooner she can move out of here and be as far away from Angelo as possible, the better. Maybe she can talk to Dave about moving into the stables. *Be serious, Elsie.*

Then she gets an idea. If she works on the tunnel now, she will be that much closer to having it finished. They already completed what she calls her little foyer and have started working on the left branch. She can keep digging back, and the sounds should be muffled. *That should be easy enough, right?* She gets up quietly and puts on her sneakers, then tiptoes past a fast-asleep Mira and scurries toward her cave. The tools are there, just waiting to be picked up again. She moves quietly and quickly. And she digs. She digs and digs with all her might, the anger of losing her memory and all of Angelo's judgmental comments coming out as she smashes rocks and impales dirt.

Elsie loses track of time and doesn't focus on how far she has gotten until she hears a voice behind her.

"What in God's name are you doing, Elsie? It's four thirty in the morning," Andrea whispers strongly.

"I am so sorry! Did I wake the children? I couldn't sleep, so I figured I would be productive."

Andrea puts a hand on Elsie's shoulder. "No, you didn't wake the children, but I'm a light sleeper and heard banging. I thought I would check it out. You need to get some sleep, or you won't be productive at all tomorrow. Why don't you come sleep on my couch? I'll curl up with Zander. He's a deep sleeper and won't wake if I crawl next to him."

"Thank you, Andrea. I am just so . . ."

And then it happens. It has been a few days since she cried, and this time it is so much more intense. Her tears flow and she cannot help herself. She begins to sob, and Andrea pulls her into her arms and holds her.

"Just let it all out, honey. You'll be stronger once it's all out."

"I hate not knowing what happened to me. I hate not knowing where I've been. I know people want answers, but I don't have them!" she whimpers.

"And by people you mean Angelo?" Andrea pulls her away to look at her.

"I understand why he is so apprehensive, but . . . it's just so hard to be here right now." Elsie continues to cry.

"I know, sweetie. Just come stay with me tonight, and tomorrow you can keep working on your room." Andrea guides her to her room and her couch, then places a blanket over Elsie and sits in a chair near the children's rooms.

"I thought you were going to sleep with Zander."

"I will. You just close your eyes and rest. You *are* safe Elsie. I promise," Andrea reassures her.

"Thank you, Andrea."

Elsie closes her eyes. It doesn't take long for her to doze off.

CHAPTER FIVE

ANGELO WAKES EARLY and sees that Elsie is gone. He quickly puts on his shoes and gets ready for his rounds, but he needs to find her first. *Who knows what she's up to?*

He goes to her "room" to see if she's there, only to find Andrea in front.

"Morning, Andrea. Have you seen Elsie?" he asks.

"Yes, she's sleeping in my room. I found her here last night working on her room, very forcefully, I might add. What did you say to her?" Andrea asks with her hands on her hips.

"I told her the truth. I don't see how she could have appeared from nowhere. It is my job to protect my family and the people of this cavern."

"And who put you in charge of protecting us? Was there a vote that I missed? Was there an election where you said, 'Anyone who comes into this cavern I will treat like crap until I get answers from them,' and then we all applauded and voted for you as our supreme protector?" she demands, speaking more acerbically than he has ever heard her.

"Why am I the only one who sees it? Why am I the only one who has questions and is on guard?" Angelo retorts.

"Why are you the only one who cannot see the pain this poor

girl is in? Why are you the only one who can't see that she has the same questions as you, but for her, not having the answers is tearing her apart?! Angelo, we appreciate that you have our best interests at heart; I think I speak for everyone here when I say that we are grateful. However, how you are treating this poor girl, you're making it harder for her to adapt when she is already lost. She can't be found until she can let her guard down, and that's impossible with you badgering her. Please, all I ask is that you show her a little grace," Andrea replies.

"Okay, okay. It's just . . . it's only a matter of time before the Elite start showing up again. It's been so long. What if they thought that if they came like it was business as usual, we would be on our best behavior and not be honest about what we're doing? So they send in one of their own that no one knows to spy on us? I trust the Elite, but only so far," Angelo explains, though the explanation sounds weak the more often he gives it.

"I can understand your point, but seriously? After all this time, you think they would just send a spy? I think you're bored and reading too many psychological thrillers," Andrea sighs. "Angelo, you are a wonderful man. You are someone we can count on and trust, but you need to get your mind right. Please. More grace." With that, Andrea marches back to her room.

Angelo stands unsure of his next move. He wants to trust Elsie; he really does. But how can he, when so many questions remain unanswered?

Perhaps kindness is the better route to getting his answers anyway.

* * *

Elsie wakes and stretches out. She can't remember the last

time she felt so rested. Andrea is there with a warm mug of water and lemon.

"You seemed to sleep well. I sent the children ahead with Marco today so you could sleep in."

Elsie jumps up, instantly frazzled. "Oh no, what time is it? I need to help with the digging. Angelo is already annoyed with me. The last thing I need is for him to think I'm slacking while others are working."

"It's okay. I spoke with him and told him you were working on your room last night and I made you sleep in here with us. He understood and felt that you should rest as long as you need to," Andrea replies.

"Are you sure it was Angelo?" Elsie frowns at her in disbelief, then sips her tea and sits back on the couch.

"Yes, Angelo. I told you he was a good guy once you get to know him. I explained to him that you are just as confused as the rest of us and he needs to back off."

"Oh, Andrea." Elsie dropped her head in her hands. "Now he's going to think I put you up to it."

"I made it clear to him that it was me telling him this and not you. Don't worry. I think you will find him more pleasant now," Andrea says with a smile.

"Thank you for the bed and the tea. I think I'll get back to work now. Otherwise, I'll be stuck in Mira's room for longer than any of us would like."

"You are more than welcome to stay here whenever you need to, Elsie." Andrea rises and embraces Elsie. "You need time to heal just like the rest of us did. Your memory will come back, and then we will all get the answers I know are inside of you."

Elsie moves out of the room and heads for her own. She finds Angelo, Marco, and Carlos all there, digging out the chamber.

"Good morning. I'm sorry I'm late," Elsie apologizes.

Angelo's unexpectedly warm smile gives her goose bumps. "It's fine. We know you needed the sleep. I hope you are well rested."

Elsie squints suspiciously at him. "You seem chipper this morning."

Angelo emerges from the opening to stand in front of her. "I realized after talking to Andrea that I have been very hard on you. I want to try to move past my opinions regarding your memory loss and work with you to try to remember what happened."

She isn't sure if this qualifies as an apology, but she will take what she can get. "Thank you, Angelo. I'll do my best to try to remember, but I'm starting to think there's a good reason I forgot it all. And I do recognize it is very suspicious. I will let you know as soon as I remember anything," Elsie promises.

"Sounds fair," Angelo answers.

"Are you two done? We have work to get to before we do our choring for the day," Marco shouts.

"Okay, okay!" Elsie calls back, smiling.

They spend the next couple of hours working on the room before Marco and Carlos leave to grab food and get to their chores. Lydia arrives at the same time to show Elsie the curtain she's working on.

"I think I just need a few more feet, and I'll be finished," Lydia says. "In the meantime, I did get inspired and started this." She holds up a light sweater in a beautiful blue color. It is short, so obviously unfinished, but it's gorgeous.

"That is truly lovely, Lydia!" Elsie remarks.

"That is a beautiful sweater," Angelo tells her. "See, you did retain what my mother taught you. We all knew you had it in you." He gives her a sideways hug.

"Thank you! I think when it's finished I'll try my hand at pants! I am not as quick as your mom, Angelo, but I promise I will get there, and everyone will have something new soon!" Lydia said, grinning widely.

Jeremy drops by soon after Lydia heads off.

"Oh, Elsie, I'm glad I found you. I finished those bars. Tell me what you think."

Elsie pops the sample into her mouth and closes her eyes with a moan.

"Jeremy, these are the best bars I have ever tasted! Thank you so much. I feel nostalgic eating them!" Elsie says as she chews another bite.

"Oh, I am so glad you like them. Here are a couple more to fuel you and the guys. I might try more fruit combinations with the ginger and ginseng. Maybe we can add new flavors into the rotation. I want to add nuts to them too, for texture."

"That's a great idea," Elsie congratulates him. He smiles as he jogs back toward the little kitchen area. Angelo, who was clearly watching them, returns to work without a word.

At one point late in the morning, Elsie runs into trouble breaking up a stone.

"Are you stuck? The rock might be too dense. Maybe move over a foot or so?" Angelo suggests.

"Nope, I am too stubborn about being symmetrical. I will get this stone to move if it takes me all day," she declares. She hammers with the pickax until Angelo takes it from her.

"Let me try." He pounds as hard as he can, and the large stone tumbles out. Behind it appears to be cement. "What the hell?" Angelo stares at it. "What is cement doing in the middle of this mountain?" He continues to hack away at the rock and dirt around the exposed cement. As he does, earth crumbles to reveal more cement behind it.

"We need to dig out more of this so we have enough room to try to break through. Maybe we can borrow a jackhammer or mallet from one of the Elite workers," Angelo says.

Elsie touches the cement. "It feels cold," she says. "I wonder what could be behind it."

"Hello! Angelo?" A woman's voice drifts into the room. Angelo walks to the opening. "Oh, hi, Simone. Thanks for coming over.

Elsie, can you come here?"

Elsie approaches cautiously. "Hi, I'm Elsie," she says, shaking the woman's hand.

"Hi, Elsie. My name is Simone. Angelo has told me a bit about you. We just ran into each other at the supply room, and he suggested I come meet you."

"*Dr.* Simone is a psychotherapist. She helps people with PTSD and other neurological conditions," Angelo explains.

Elsie eyes them both sternly. "I am not crazy."

"No one said you were, Elsie. A lot of people experience trauma, and often the only way their brains know how to deal with it is to forget what happened to them. I help them recollect those memories and then confront them."

"Dr. Simone helped us all make the transition into our new lives," Angelo explains. "Everyone was a mess, and she helped us all get through it emotionally. There is nothing wrong with talking to someone."

"I don't need a shrink." Elsie folds her arms stubbornly.

Angelo gently pulls her to the side and whispers, "I told you I would help you try to remember. Work with Simone. This is your best bet."

Elsie finally relaxes her shoulders and sighs, realizing she needs to do this. "Okay, I'll try. But if I start hating my parents or something like that, I'm out! This is strictly for remembering the past five years," she declares.

"Agreed." Angelo nods. "Okay, Simone, she is willing."

"Great," Dr. Simone says. "Just so you know how I work, Elsie, I use techniques like meditation and hypnosis to bring memories to the surface. It will just be you and me in the room. Hopefully we can unlock what's buried inside that memory bank of yours." The doctor touches Elsie's arm reassuringly. "How about we start tomorrow around lunchtime?"

"Okay," Elsie agrees. "I'll meet you at the far tables in the main part of the cavern."

"Great. See you then. Bye, Angelo." Simone walks off, waving over her shoulder.

"Well, she seems like a very nice and smart woman." Elsie narrows her eyes at Angelo as they make for the tables where Marco and Carlos are settled.

"And married to Brian, a former police officer. Why do you sound like Mira, trying to couple me off with someone?" Angelo asks.

"I don't know," Elsie says automatically, then scoffs, "That's a lie; I do know. I figure if you partner up with someone, you'll get off my back."

Angelo laughs. "That's probably the same answer Mira would give me."

She's pleasantly surprised by his lighthearted demeanor and smiles back as they sit at the table. "Oh, Jeremy gave me enough of these fig and honey bars for everyone to try. Here." She passes out the bars.

Angelo tries it first. "Is this with the ginger and ginseng?"

"It is. What do you think?"

"It's good. This will definitely help get us through that cement wall." He gives Elsie an admiring nod. She blushes and smiles back.

"Cement wall?" Marco asks just as Mira and Andrea join them, bringing fruit and cereal that they offer the others.

"Elsie met Dr. Simone," Angelo volunteers to everyone. "She has agreed to meet with her to try to unlock some of her missing memories."

"Yes, we'll see if it works," Elsie adds, a little annoyed that her visit to a shrink is being publicized.

"Dr. Simone is awesome. She worked wonders with all of us when we realized we were stuck here," Mira gushes.

Marco seems intent on rewinding the conversation. "Wait, guys, what cement?"

"Yes, she was a huge help to the children and me. She helped me through the loss of my husband and to begin moving forward here with the children. I don't know if I would have made it without her," Andrea says. Marco coughs as though choking on his water. "She wasn't the only one to help us through everything," she adds, blushing, and looks down at her fruit.

"I think if anyone can get through the block in your memories, it's Dr. Simone. She is so patient and kind in her approach." Mira says.

"Fingers crossed. I think we'll all sleep better once we get some answers. I mean that in a good way, Elsie," Angelo says. "Well, we better get back to digging Elsie's cave. Oh, that reminds me! Marco, Carlos, we exposed a cement wall in the back of the new chamber."

Marco throws his arms up.

"What? Cement? That doesn't make any sense," Carlos says.

"Maybe there was another tunnel or partial subway built in the mountain before all this happened?" Marco offers.

"Can't be; nothing was built in this mountain. That's why the Elite chose it, I bet. It couldn't be compromised when they started building," Carlos replies.

"Well, it is there, and there must be something behind it. I intend to find out. Do we have a jackhammer or something that can break through cement?" Angelo asks.

"We don't have anything that can bust up a cement wall other than large mallets and brute force. Maybe if we all take a go at it, we can do some damage," Carlos says.

"Well, there's only a small part exposed right now. Why don't we remove as much dirt as we can? I want to make sure whatever is behind there is big enough to be worth the effort. It won't do much good to smash through something small."

Angelo's logic is sound. They all swiftly go their separate ways, clearly excited to learn what is behind the cement wall. So much so that it becomes the talk of the cavern. While the men and Elsie dig, everyone passes by to check it out, making some excuse or another. Elsie and the wall are the most thrilling things to appear in a long while.

"So, Elsie, what were you studying in college? You mentioned you had an internship?" Angelo asks as they work.

"I majored in business with a minor in human relations. I wanted to be a mediator," Elsie replies.

Angelo nods. "That makes a lot of sense."

"Why do you say that?"

"You're good with people. You show no reservations when it comes to dealing with them." His dark eyes meet hers, and her cheeks grow warm. "What else did you enjoy doing? Or were you one of those students that hung out in their dorm room studying all the time?"

"No, I was a good student, but I had my fun. I was the fundraiser leader of my sorority."

Angelo's laughter interrupts her.

"You were a sorority girl? I didn't expect that!"

"I put together some really fun events for fundraising, I will have you know. And it was a small sorority."

"What kind of fundraisers did you do?" Marco asks.

"The usual silly stuff like bake sales, dances, talent shows . . . and Jell-O wrestling," Elsie lists.

"Jell-O wrestling?" Marco cackles. "Who would wrestle? The sisters?"

"There was a fraternity we ran certain fundraisers with, so we would have four pools filled with Jell-O, two for the guys and two for the girls. It was one of our top fundraisers," Elsie declares proudly.

"I bet," Angelo says. "I'm sure there were many more spectators around the women's pools than the guys."

Elsie grins. "How did you know?"

They expose a little more of the wall before they call it a day and head over to dinner. Elsie feels like she's made headway with Angelo. She enjoyed opening up a little more and experiencing his more easygoing side.

✦ ✦ ✦

"You sure turned a corner with Elsie," Marco says to Angelo when Elsie gets up to get more waffles for the table. "You two haven't stopped talking since we got back to the cave."

"Really?" Mira leans into Marco. "Do tell! What have they been talking about?"

"The stuff people talk about when they're trying to get to know each other. Favorite books, movies, music, ya know."

"Well, do you know all that about Andrea? Haven't you two talked about that stuff?" Angelo asks Marco, feeling strangely flustered.

He enjoyed getting to know Elsie today and looks forward to knowing her better. Even he couldn't help but notice the sadness in her eyes when she spoke of her family and friends at school. It was a fresh, painful sadness, as if she were grieving for the first time. He wanted so badly to help her somehow, to hold her. Instead, he changed the subject. She seemed to know he was doing so for her benefit.

Elsie is proving to be someone of interest, but for all the right reasons. Angelo is afraid that if he does finally let his guard down, that will be the moment the terrible truth about her comes out; yet it would be so easy to let his guard down.

"Yes, they have, and we know how Marco feels about her. Should we assume the same for you?" Mira raises her eyebrows.

"Assume what about whom?" Elsie asks as she sits.

The three answer in unison: "Nothing."

"Well, that wasn't suspicious at all."

"Just talking about what we think is behind the wall," Mira chirps.

"I think it's an ancient bedroom or tomb!" Amanda comes to the table, plopping right between Angelo and Elsie. Elsie moves over to make room on the bench.

"I don't think they had cement in ancient times," Elsie comments. "Unless you consider the nineteenth century ancient."

"Well, it must be something old, or it wouldn't be hidden so deep in the mountain," Amanda declares.

"It can't be that old. I'm sure the Elite have something to do with it," Angelo says. He decides to shift topics. "Speaking of ancient, Amanda, Elsie likes the same classic movie that you do! She said it's one of her favorites."

"Yes, I love a good love story when someone is down and out but is still good and karma rewards them with love," Elsie explains.

Amanda giggles. "Oh, that's cute. I just love that she meets a rich guy who spoils her rotten."

"Well, I think anyone would spoil Julia Roberts regardless of her occupation," Angelo says.

Elsie smiles slyly. "She's no Taylor Swift."

"Hey, don't start that! I told you it's all Mira's fault!" Angelo says defensively.

Elsie laughs. "I would have never guessed that Angelo was a Swifty!"

"It is really my fault. Ever since I heard her songs redone, I was hooked, and Angelo suffered the most. He had to take me to concerts and listen to her songs in the car. It was inevitable he would be a fan!" Mira explains.

They all laugh with the exception of Amanda, who seems uncomfortable. "Angelo, I think the new crop will be ready soon, and I was hoping you could help me with the corn and wheat. You know I'm all thumbs when it comes to that."

"I can see if one of the other guys is available. I really want to get moving on the cement wall tomorrow. Is that okay?" he asks, growing tired of fending her off.

"Sure," Amanda says shortly. She rises. "I guess I'll see you later."

"You really are oblivious, aren't you?" Mira sighs when Amanda is gone.

"He really is," Elsie laughs.

"What? I want to get through the wall tomorrow. I don't think my time should be wasted helping her with something she really doesn't need help with."

"Oh, so you aren't so oblivious?" Elsie asks.

"I will not date someone for the sake of it. There are more important things to be done than worry about hooking up with someone," Angelo says, extremely uncomfortable to be having this conversation with Elsie of all people.

"Well, let me know what time you want to get started tomorrow." Elsie gets up as well. "I'm going to visit with Andrea before bedtime."

"First thing in the morning. Don't forget you told Simone you would see her as well," Angelo says.

"Yes, yes, I know. I'll meet with her, I promise. See you later."

* * *

Marco stops at the entrance of Andrea's cave while Andrea and Elsie are chatting. As much as Andrea enjoys this new friendship and the new whirl of gossip and intrigue Elsie has brought to her life, she wishes Elsie weren't here to witness the awkwardness with Marco.

"Hello, Andrea. I was wondering if the kids wanted to kick the ball around a bit. I have a little time before bed," he says, looking hesitant.

"They've actually settled down for the night, Marco," Andrea says apologetically. "Maybe tomorrow? I know they love playing soccer with you." She hopes he sees how much she appreciates him.

"Oh, okay, sure. Well, good night, you two." Marco goes to leave, but Elsie rises.

"Wait, Marco, I was going to turn in for the night anyway. Why don't you keep Andrea company for a bit before settling in? See you tomorrow, Andrea." Elsie winks at her and is gone before Andrea can protest.

"Oh, is that okay with you, Andrea?" Marco asks.

"Of course it is. Come have a seat."

Marco takes Elsie's place on the couch, and Andrea stays in the chair, doing her best to smile normally.

"How was your day? The kids seemed to enjoy the garden," Marco says.

"Yes, they love working there. Especially Zander, since it's new to him. I think they love the animals more, but we can't work in just one place."

Marco moves to the end of the couch closer to Andrea's chair.

"Look, I know we've talked about a lot of things from our past, but—"

Andrea swiftly cuts him off.

"Please, don't. I have expressed to you before my concerns."

"Yes, you are older than I am, but things are different now. I am a man, not a boy who just plays with your kids. My feelings have grown."

"Marco, you have a crush that you are mistaking for feelings. You have been a wonderful help to me. You have become one of my closest friends, but we have to accept this for what it is: friendship."

"I know you have feelings for me too."

Irritated because he's right but he should know better than to push, she insists, "No. I love you as my friend. I always will. Nothing more, nothing less."

Marco stands to leave. "I'm sorry I bothered you tonight," he says stiffly. "I just thought, well, apparently it doesn't matter what I think, as it is just foolish childhood fantasies."

"That is not what I said, Marco," Andrea stands as well and reaches for his hand, grasping it. He turns to her and comes close, so close she can feel his breath on her lips.

"What are you saying then? If I am not a foolish child, then what am I?" He leans in closer so that their foreheads meet. Andrea's breathing quickens.

"I'm saying that you are my best friend, and we can't confuse that with anything else. For the sake of my children. I must be responsible." She falters and closes her eyes. "Please, Marco, don't. I can't."

Marco turns away. "Good night, Andrea. I'll come get the children tomorrow and bring them to the garden so that you can have a little time for yourself—to think." He gives her a meaningful look before leaving.

Andrea's chest rises quickly from the encounter. Of course she loves Marco, and it scares her. He is so much younger than she is. Would the children be confused? They truly do look to Marco as an older brother—someone to emulate and play with, not obey.

If she acted on her feelings, if she kissed him, there would be no going back. She must be more careful in the future.

* * *

Elsie passes her cave and ducks inside on an impulse, placing her hand against the cement. She closes her eyes and senses something familiar, but she can't quite place it. She turns to leave and runs into Dr. Simone.

"Oh, hello, Elsie, I was just taking a walk. I couldn't sleep," Dr. Simone says.

"I was just on my way to Mira's cave, but I'm not really sleepy either. Do you think I could walk with you? Get to know you before you poke around in my brain?" Elsie asks.

"It would be a pleasure." Dr. Simone gestures ahead, and they walk the perimeter of the cave—at first in silence, but then Elsie breaks it.

"How long did you study psychotherapy?"

"Well, I got my doctorate about fifteen years ago and worked at some counseling centers as a therapist. I opened my own practice about a decade ago and started practicing hypnosis therapy. I was getting brilliant results, so I perfected it, and the rest is history," Simone explains.

"Do you find hypnosis works better than meditation?" Elsie asks.

"I find they are really one and the same. Through hypnosis, there is a tendency to become more lost in the memory, where with meditation, you feel more present. I think most people prefer meditation when dealing with issues of control. Those who really want to dig deep will be all in with hypnosis. It really depends on the patient."

"I'm worried that the memories that come up will be from my past with my family and friends. Not that I'm worried to remember them. But it is a deep sorrow I don't want to get lost in," Elsie admits.

"Maybe those memories need to come forth in order for you to remember what happened afterward," the doctor suggests. "If those memories come up, we will deal with them. We'll take it one day at a time."

They stop in front of Angelo's, Mira's, and Marco's rooms.

"This is me. I'll see you tomorrow."

"It was a pleasure talking with you, Elsie. Don't worry. I am confident we will get to the bottom of it. Have a good night." Dr. Simone continues her walk.

"Did you start your session early?" Angelo asks as Elsie enters the suite.

"No, she was taking a stroll, so I joined her. I figured if I got to talking with her a bit, I would feel more comfortable getting 'shrinked,'" Elsie says with air quotes.

"Not a bad idea. I'll see you at your cave tomorrow after my rounds. Night, Elsie," Angelo says almost tenderly.

"Good night, Angelo," Elsie replies. She enters Mira's room to find Mira already asleep on the floor. Elsie shakes her head at the kindness of this woman.

Elsie lies on the mattress, staring at the ceiling. *A lot happened today.* She got a therapist, made some new friends, and even made a friend out of Angelo. She smiles at the thought of him. Something about him makes her limbs tingle. She briefly imagines what it would be like to kiss him, touch him, then shakes her head. In the end, Angelo still doesn't trust her. Plus, Amanda has made clear her intentions with Angelo, and Elsie doesn't need the drama. *And why isn't he interested in Amanda? Amanda is pretty, and she seems nice enough when she doesn't have her hackles up.*

* * *

Angelo wakes with a jolt once again, overwhelmed by a sense of loss and confusion. *Why does my chest hurt?* He feels like he lost Elsie, and it is a feeling he doesn't like in the slightest. He slides to his feet and tiptoes to Mira's room, relieved beyond measure to see Elsie sleeping on the mattress. Mira is on the floor. He shakes his head; Mira has always been such a good soul.

He thinks about how Mira clung so quickly to Elsie. He shouldn't be surprised. Her caring heart and willingness to give of herself never wavers. It is why she was going to nursing school before the world ended. She puts her trust in people first and lets them prove her wrong later, a quality that worries him even as it makes him proud.

As he gazes at Elsie, the feelings and urges from his dream war with his mistrust. Is it safe to let his guard down? Is she really all she says she is? *Only* what she says she is? Is someone looking for her?

He returns to his little room and his recliner, closing his eyes only to see visions of Elsie, filling him with the need to make her feel safe and secure with him. God, he hopes Dr. Simone can get those memories back. Once she has those, they can move forward to . . . Well, they can move forward.

CHAPTER SIX

ELSIE, ANGELO, AND Carlos work the entire morning to expose the cement, finally deciding there's enough visible to be worth working on the wall itself after lunch. Elsie grabs her fig bar and heads off to meet with Dr. Simone in the grand meeting room, though she wishes she suggested a more private location.

"Hello, Elsie. How are you feeling this morning?" Dr. Simone greets her.

"Okay, all things considered. How do we get started?" Elsie asks, wanting to get the experience over with. The doctor doesn't seem to take offense at her terseness.

"I want you to close your eyes and take deep breaths. I will count to three about five times. I want you to think of the colors of the rainbow in order: red, orange, yellow, green, blue, and indigo. Think of each color as you add it to your rainbow. Once your rainbow is completed, I want you to build it again and again, until your mind goes where it needs to go. Ready?" Dr. Simone explains.

"Let's do this." Elsie straightens and closes her eyes, listening to Dr. Simone count. She layers colors one on top of the other, just as Dr. Simone described. She builds about three rainbows before she finds herself in a white room, sitting in a chair.

There is a man, but his face is fuzzy. He sits across from her, removing a needle from her arm.

"How are you feeling today, Elsie?" he asks.

"I'm well. I think you've taken more blood from me than I can restore before lunch though." She laughs. She knows this man and is comfortable with him.

"I promise you it will replenish itself before lunchtime," he says. "I was thinking we could grab lunch together and talk about how you got here. I'm still in awe that you were able to sleep in the hardware store for as many days as you did."

"I am so tired of talking about it. Can we just talk about something else? Like what our lives were like before this? Can we just pretend to be normal people living in a normal world?" Elsie asks, her eyes batting like a manipulative debutant.

He laughs, "You know that won't work on me. We aren't normal people living normal lives, Elsie. We have lost people, a lot of people, and we need to find a way to not lose more. I really think you can help with that."

"I know, but . . ."

Elsie's mind gets hazy, like it has hit a wall. She cries out, "Wait! Don't go!" but is immediately brought back to the cavern, sitting across from Dr. Simone.

"How much of that did you get?" Elsie asks.

"I can only hear your side, what you are speaking. What did you see?" Dr. Simone asks.

Elsie tells her about the vision. "I couldn't see his face, and I don't know what time frame I was in. I assume it was after the bombs hit, but how do I know for sure?"

"We don't know for sure. We would have to dig deeper. As you do, you should be able to start describing what is going on and what is being said to you so that I can help you along. For now, I don't want to overload your brain or stress your body out. We will continue tomorrow if that is alright. I'll leave it up to you if you want to fill the others in. I won't tell them any of what we learn together," Dr. Simone informs her.

"I appreciate that. I'll probably tell Angelo just so he doesn't think I'm hiding anything. The more I can tell him, the easier it is for him to trust me."

"I think that is wise; however, it is your decision. This is your mind and your memories. They belong to you," Dr. Simone assures her.

"I appreciate that very much, Dr. Simone. I'll see you again tomorrow."

Elsie stands and moves toward the tunnel, where she finds Angelo waiting. He straightens from where he was leaning against the wall.

"How did it go? How do you feel?"

"Good. I remembered something. I can't place the where, with who, or when, but I was talking to someone who drew blood from me. That's weird, right?"

"The person drew blood from you? That is weird, but I'm sure it will make sense eventually."

Elsie smiles. "That means a lot coming from you. I appreciate it."

Marco approaches them, rubbing his hands together. "So, I hear we're busting down a wall today!"

Angelo rolls his eyes, and they all head to the garden room to collect the new tools they'll need. "Well, we're going to start, though I don't know how far we'll get. It depends on how thick it is."

"I can't wait to see if it's a secret laboratory from a medieval scientist!" Marco says.

"You've been down here too long," says Elsie. "It's probably just a tunnel to the garden."

"Nope, it is in completely the wrong position," Marco corrects her.

"Well, let's stop talking about it and start working on it," Angelo says as he grabs a mallet and hands it to Marco, then hefts another one for himself. "Elsie, can you work on removing more dirt? If this does end up being nothing, you still need a room to live in."

"Aye aye, Captain." Elsie salutes him.

They head back to Elsie's cave and spend the next few hours trying to break through the wall but manage only a few splinters and cracks. It is clearly thick. Angelo estimates aloud that it will probably take another few days to get through—if they even can.

"Are there any priests or rabbis here?" Elsie suddenly asks as they work. "I haven't seen signs of religion."

Angelo frowns. "Are you looking for religion, Elsie? No, there are no priests or rabbis. I think many of them stayed with their congregations, churches, temples—you know, the whole captain going down with the ship thing. Everyone keeps to themselves down here when it comes to religion and praying and such."

"Have you thought of creating something nondenominational?" Elsie asks.

"By all means, if you want something started, go for it," Marco says.

"I wasn't a good Christian in the way of going to services or anything like that. I celebrated the major holidays. This situation just strikes me as one where people would need God the most," Elsie says.

Angelo shrugs one shoulder as he pauses in his hammering. "Most people gave up on religion and God when they lost the ones they loved and their normal lives."

"Yes, but she saved you all by guiding you here, right?"

"She?" Marco chuckles.

Elsie smiles, ignoring his sarcasm. "Yes, she. I think the 'He, Him, Father' thing was because the writings were done by men."

Angelo laughs. "You sound like my mother. She never gave up on God, telling us that we were saved through his mercy and such. Though she did say 'Him,' not 'Her.' We followed her lead in prayers, but when she was gone, I was done. I didn't have much faith after that."

"We all feel that way," Marco says soberly.

"That makes sense. I was just curious. I'm trying hard to bring back my memories, and it has gotten me thinking about things that I miss from life before all this. Maybe we can have a party. Create our own holiday that is nonreligious and just a celebration of the life we have here. What do you think?" Elsie suggests.

"That sounds like fun, but what would we celebrate with? We have no clothes, no party foods, no decorations. What would be the point?" Marco asks.

"Well, I can ask Jeremy for suggestions on food. Maybe he can make something special. The kids can make decorations out of whatever we can find here. Maybe Lydia can make some special shirts for everyone to wear. We can call it Cavern Day and just celebrate! We have music saved on our phones; I'm sure we can create a playlist. Please?" she begs the brothers.

"Sounds good in theory. Let me talk to the rest of the leaders. If everyone is on board, you can talk to the others to see what they think. Does that sound fair?" Angelo offers.

"I think that sounds wonderful!" Elsie says, smiling brightly. She's thrilled when he smiles back abruptly, almost like he can't help himself.

* * *

Elsie again sits at a table with Mira, Marco, Andrea, and the children. Tonight they are having pea soup, which is delicious. Jeremy works wonders with what he has. A young woman approaches as they eat. Brunette and brown-eyed, she wears an uneasy smile.

"Hello. Elsie, right?" she asks.

"Hey, Hope. Yes, this is Elsie. Elsie, this is Hope," Mira says, eyeing her curiously.

"Elsie, can I speak with you alone? I think we have a couple things in common, and I would love to get to know you," Hope says.

"You are more than welcome to join us, Hope," Andrea offers.

Hope shifts from foot to foot. "I was hoping Elsie and I could just chat for a bit, if that's okay."

"Sure, of course," Elsie says. "I'll be back for games in a bit."

Elsie rises with her bowl and follows Hope to an empty table on the fringes.

"This is a little far. Is everything okay?" Elsie asks.

"I needed to talk to you after what happened to you in the garden cavern. With Mike," Hope says.

"I didn't do anything to him that he didn't deserve," Elsie says fiercely, setting her food on the table. "He came on to me. I swear, if you both are together—"

"Oh God no, it's nothing like that!" Hope sighs heavily. As they sit, she stares at her bowl of soup. "About a year ago, I was in the greenhouse watering the plants. I was alone, unexpectedly; that doesn't usually happen. I think Andrea was supposed to be in there with the kids, but one of them had a bad cold or something." She meets Elsie's eyes. "Mike was fixing a sprinkler, and he got to talking to me. I laughed at a joke he made, and he took that as an invitation."

Elsie puts her hand over Hope's.

"I haven't told anyone. I was so embarrassed. He came up to me and started kissing me. I backed away, and he told me we were alone and I didn't have to worry about what anyone thought. He grabbed my arm and started touching me, my breasts, my butt as he continued to kiss me. I asked him to stop, I tried to get away, but he had me by my waist, and he wouldn't let go. He said he knew I wanted this as badly as he did. Thank God someone came into the greenhouse. I didn't even see who it was because he let go and I ran out of there. I try to avoid being in any rooms he's in now."

"Oh my God, Hope. I am so sorry." Elsie considers how to phrase her question so that it doesn't sound accusatory. "Why haven't you told anyone?" In general she knows why women often do not speak of these things, but the people here seem kind and understanding.

"Because he's the head electrician. He would probably just say I'm making up the whole thing, and everyone would look at me differently. Anyway, I just wanted to thank you for putting him in his place," Hope finishes.

"Have you heard of him doing anything to anyone else around here?" Elsie asks.

"He flirts, but I haven't heard of him getting physical with anyone. I try to make sure that no one is alone with him. I make rounds and check where he is. Most of the time, he's with the other guy, Bart, so I don't worry too much."

"We should tell Angelo. He should know this guy is a loose cannon," Elsie suggests, regretting telling Angelo to drop the issue.

"No! Please don't tell anyone, Elsie, please! I don't want anyone knowing what happened to me. Really, it was nothing in the end."

"But if someone hadn't come in—"

"But someone did. They usually do. No one is ever really alone around here. Just watch your back, and thank you. That's all I wanted to say."

Hope stands and hurries away to dispose of her bowl in the dish bin. Elsie rises slowly, taken aback by what she just heard. She assumed Mike went after her because she's the new girl. She should have guessed there was a pattern. She will honor Hope's wishes, though, and not tell anyone about Hope's part of it.

She returns to the others after tossing her own bowl in the dish bin. The children seem to be winning against Marco and Andrea in Monopoly.

Mira turns to Elsie. "What was that about?"

"She heard I was from Dallas and wanted to see if I knew anyone she knew." She hates lying to Mira.

Angelo joins the group, sitting next to his sister.

"I saw you talking to Hope. Everything okay?"

Mira rescues her. "Always investigating. Geez, Angelo, can't the girl make new friends without you breathing down her neck?" she scolds him.

Angelo shakes his head. "Always yelling at me when I'm trying to make conversation. Why do you have to make everything into an issue?"

"Because I know you. You are never just trying to make conversation. If you were, then you would go sit with Amanda."

"Nice, Mira. Elsie, what games do you like to play?"

"I like trivia and word games like Scrabble. I was addicted to crosswords too."

"I love trivia games as well. See, Mira, I do know how to make conversation. Maybe one day we can play a trivia game. I am sure I will win," Angelo gloats as Mira rolls her eyes.

"Please, I hope you have met your match with Elsie. I can't beat him to save my life," Mira giggles.

"We will have to see. I am pretty good." Elsie smiles. "After the day I had today, though, I think I'm going to sleep. I'm pooped."

"Okay, I'll join in a little bit. I want to see who wins this little war over here. These guys keep hoping to beat the kids, but they never do," Mira says with relish.

Angelo watches Elsie stand. "Good night, Elsie."

"Good night, everyone." Elsie waves as she retires for the evening.

* * *

The next day, after everyone leaves to do their chores, Elsie decides to visit the barn. Next week she will be in the rotation of chores, and she wants to familiarize herself with the tasks in each section. The barn is the obvious first choice.

She observes how everyone is working, whether they're cleaning the stables, feeding the animals, sorting through the eggs; she even jumps in from time to time to help. This is their survival, and she wants to feel a part of it, not singled out from it.

She returns to the main cavern at lunchtime, grabs an apple, and meets Dr. Simone at the same table as yesterday.

"How are you doing today, Elsie?" the doctor asks.

"I'm doing very well, actually. I had a really nice morning in the barn area, and I feel I'm making good progress with everyone here. So far, so good," Elsie replies.

"That's great. Having your mind in a comfortable place might help bring your memories forward easier. Are you ready to start?" Dr. Simone asks.

"Yes." Elsie places her apple aside and sits with her hands on her knees. She takes deep breaths. Dr. Simone begins her counting, and Elsie builds her rainbow.

Elsie is sitting in a patch of purple flowers. She remembers learning in a botany course that if the flower smells edible, it most likely is. Flowers that have a foul smell are dangerous to eat and most likely poisonous. This purple flower has a light fragrance, not foul at all.

Elsie feels in her gut that she can eat this flower, so she takes a petal and places it in her mouth. It tastes fine—nothing exciting or mouthwatering about it, but it is something to eat. She waits a few minutes, and when nothing happens, she decides to take some for the road. She picks a bundle and places them in her knapsack. Just then, a man approaches her. He has light-brown hair, fair skin, and dark-brown eyes. He is smiling as he jogs up to her.

"Elsie! There's a huge apple tree behind this house! I filled my bag, so we're set for a little while at least."

Elsie looks around now and sees she is in the garden of a small house. It looks cozy, a place she can see herself living in. "Why don't we stay here, Max? I'm so tired. I just want to rest," Elsie complains.

"We can't. It's a matter of time before the bombs start coming inland. We can't be anywhere near a target."

"But this is such a quiet little town. Why would they bomb it?" Elsie asks.

"We're still too close to a major city. We have to move to the mountains," Max reminds her.

"Yes, yes. Okay. I found these flowers. They're edible, so I thought we could take some."

"The day I start eating flowers is the day I know I'm almost dead!" Max laughs.

"Well, I'll eat them. And I'll take some roots so we can plant them up in the mountains too. Hopefully they can flourish there."

"I doubt anything will flourish," he says, looking eastward with a gloomy expression.

"Well, I'm glad we found each other. Thank you for dragging me out." Elsie smiles at him with the utmost gratitude.

"It's just lucky I heard you crying. Let's go," he says brusquely. "You know I hate staying anywhere too long."

Elsie briefly studies Max. She has no romantic feelings toward him. She means it when she says she is grateful to him for saving her, but she knows her days are numbered nonetheless. She hopes they go together. She gathers more of the purple flowers and stuffs them into her bag, then stands and walks with Max.

Her vision goes fuzzy but then becomes clear again. She and Max are sitting under a willow tree. The leaves are dying, which is odd considering the summer season. They sit in the shade, and Elsie has her head on Max's shoulder. She eats some of the purple flowers as Max eats an apple. He begins to cough and has trouble stopping.

"Are you choking? Are you okay, Max?" Elsie asks in a panic.

In between coughs, he answers, "I'm okay. Not choking. My chest just feels tight."

Elsie hugs him, frightened. In their travels she has witnessed many people coughing uncontrollably and then collapsing, dead. She can't lose Max. What would she do without him? He stops coughing and stands.

"The faster we get to the mountains, the faster we can escape this hellscape."

Elsie rises and joins hands with him.

Her mind goes fuzzy again, and now she's in a street, and Max is coughing uncontrollably. She rubs his back, crying and asking him to hold on.

"Please, Max, just try to hold on. We'll find a house. We can stay there; please just hold on and come with me." She tries to walk, but Max falls to his knees. He meets her imploring gaze and presses his hand to her cheek, wiping away her tears with his thumb. He coughs one last time and falls, staring up at the sky. He is unmoving. He has stopped breathing.

Elsie cries and lies next to him, waiting for her turn.

Then Elsie opens her eyes, tears streaming from them. Gradually Dr. Simone's concerned expression comes into focus.

"You were able to describe what happened. I heard everything, not just your side of the conversation. This is great progress for your second day, Elsie. How are you feeling right now?"

"I-I think I need to lie down for a bit. Dr. Simone, can you let Angelo know what happened? I don't think I can describe that again."

"Of course, Elsie, if that is what you would like me to do."

"Yes, please. If anyone needs me, I'll be in Mira's room." Elsie stands, her legs wobbly. Dr. Simone quickly rises to help to steady her.

"I'll be okay. I just need a little while to myself. Thank you."

* * *

Angelo finds Elsie sobbing on Mira's mattress.

He kneels beside her. "Elsie, are you okay? Dr. Simone just spoke to me."

"Yes." Elsie sits up, tears flowing from her eyes. "It's just . . . I still don't remember it. I felt like I was watching a movie. Right now, as I replay it in my mind, it's like watching a rerun. I still don't *feel* it. I am so scared, Angelo."

Angelo enfolds her in an embrace. He then pulls away and looks at her. "It will all be okay. We'll figure this out. Maybe this is the memory you needed to bring up because you blocked it all out, and you're still trying to block it out." *It would be so easy to kiss her right now,* he thinks, and is immediately annoyed at the intrusive thought. Their faces are only inches apart.

"I don't know," she whispers. "This feels different. Like, I remember yesterday, the day before, and so on. I remember what I ate, what I did, but this, it doesn't feel like anything." She puts her head in her hands. "I feel lost."

Mira enters. "Elsie! Marco just told me you had a rough session. I am so sorry!" She pushes Angelo out of the way to sit next to Elsie and curl an arm around her. "Do you know who that was? Was he a relative or a friend?"

"I don't think he was related to me. I think he was someone I met during the crisis. I honestly can't remember him. Isn't that so sad? That I would forget someone who apparently meant so much to me? I feel like a horrible person."

"Don't you think that way at all!! Who knows what happened to you afterward. My heart is breaking for you right now." Mira holds Elsie as she begins to cry again.

"Well, Mira, it seems you've got this," Angelo says, uncomfortable and unsure what to do.

"Okay, I think it best that Elsie just chills here for the rest of the day and night," she says to Angelo. She turns back to Elsie. "I'll bring you dinner, and then we can just veg out here and play some card games or something. How does that sound?" Mira offers.

"That sounds great. I don't think I want to face anyone else right now."

* * *

Elsie is swimming near a waterfall, wearing only a bra and underwear. Suddenly there is a splash, and she is covered in waves. She rights herself and yells, "Max! You're such a jerk." She splashes him as he laughs.

"How could you not know I was going to cannonball into this gorgeous lake? It was practically begging for it!"

"A heads-up would have been nice!" Elsie gazes up at the waterfall. "It really is beautiful. I wish we could camp out here for the night."

"Why don't we? We can take cover in the cave and sleep. Then in the morning we can start out again," Max suggests.

"Really, could we? I think it would be perfect. The sound of the waterfall could definitely lull us to sleep, so long as no animals come to disturb us."

"Nothing dangerous here anyway. Probably some deer and smaller animals like raccoons and rabbits. Maybe we could set a trap and have them for dinner!" Max's eyes light up. "I'm going to see what I can use for a trap. You relax here. Meet you by the oak in a little bit." He paddles back to shore.

Elsie floats along. It is so peaceful here and perfect. After everything they have been through, this is the best thing that they could have stumbled across.

Suddenly, Elsie hears explosions in the distance. She flounders to the edge of the lake and sees Max running back to her, grabbing their clothing.

"Let's go, Elsie! We have to get moving. They're dropping more bombs!" he shouts.

"No!" Elsie begins to cry. "Why can't we just have one night where we aren't running and moving? I want to stay, Max. Maybe if we get deep enough in that cave and hide out now, we won't be affected."

"Don't be silly, Elsie, we have to run!" Max yells as the eruptions get closer. In the distance she hears screams and yelling.

"Please, Max. We can't outrun the bombs," Elsie pleads. Max looks into her eyes. He gives in.

"If we smell fire close, we are outta here!"

* * *

Elsie jumps up, breathing heavily. It seems the memory of Max's death is bringing up other memories as well.

"Oh good, you're awake," Mira says, peeking into the room. "I brought us some goodies. Well, if apple muffins are considered goodies. We have oatmeal for dinner because I refuse to call it porridge and then some apple muffins for dessert. Jeremy only made enough for everyone to have one, but that's better than none, I say!" Mira sounds very excited, and Elsie struggles to orient herself to the evening after the desperate circumstances of her dream.

Elsie thinks of telling Mira about the potential memory, but she wants to hold on to it for now. It didn't solve any mysteries of who she was or how she got there, after all.

"Thanks, it looks great," Elsie says instead.

"Any thought to who that guy was in your memory?" Mira asks, almost as if she knows Elsie is hiding something more.

"No," Elsie answers honestly, "still no clue." She pokes at her oatmeal. She appreciates having food, but the sparse fruit doesn't hide that it's still oatmeal, one of her least favorite foods growing up.

"You'll get there eventually."

Angelo enters holding up a box. "Look what I found on the bottom of the game shelf. Trivial Pursuit! I thought we could play to get your mind off things."

"That is really sweet, Angelo, but no one is as good as you at knowing useless knowledge," Mira jokes.

"Actually," Elsie interjects, "it might do me some good to access that part of my memory so I don't feel completely useless."

"That's true, and maybe it will get your memory train rolling!" Mira says, perking up. "Okay, Angelo, good job. Let's set it up."

They play for an hour, and Elsie is indeed good at the game. She and Angelo are pretty evenly matched. They both have only one pie slice each to gain, while Mira still has three. Each time Mira gets a question wrong, the two of them answer correctly simultaneously. Mira rolls her eyes continuously.

"Okay, I am done! I'm going to see if anyone passed on the apple muffins and snag us a couple more." She grins. "You can keep asking each other trivia questions and see who answers the most. I can't keep up with you!" Mira leaves them alone.

"How are you feeling?" Angelo asks.

"Better now. I just wish I could *remember* remember, you know what I mean?" Elsie says.

"It will come to you. You just need more time." He starts to clear up the game, and Elsie helps. They brush hands in the process and lock eyes.

"Elsie," he breathes.

"Angelo," she answers. She allows her hand to linger over his, sending a bloom of heat through her body. Should she lean in, pull back? *What is he thinking?*

"I want . . ." Angelo looks down. "I want to apologize for my behavior when you first arrived. I just want us all to be safe, and it wasn't fair for me—"

"That was a lifetime ago. I don't blame you for your suspicions, and I don't want to dwell on the past. Let's just move forward." Elsie catches his gaze again.

Mira beams as she enters the room. "Yes! I scored us each one more! Thank goodness not everyone likes apples as much as I do." She pauses. "Did I just interrupt something?"

Angelo laughs. "In fact you're just in time to help clean up. I'm tired, so I'm going to sleep. Good night, ladies." He stands and exits.

"I did just interrupt, didn't I?" Mira asks Elsie.

"Just two friends cleaning up a board game."

Mira gives Elsie the side-eye. "Okay, sure, whatever you say."

Before bed they chat about what they were doing right before the bombs hit as they eat their muffins. Mira misses nursing school, and Elsie wishes she knew how she did on her exams.

Elsie insists on taking the floor. As Mira shuts the lamp off, Elsie prays for uneventful sleep. No memories, no dreams, just sleep.

* * *

"How did you sleep?" Mira asks first thing the next morning.

"I dreamed we were all on *Jeopardy* and Angelo was dominating the board. So I guess last night's distraction worked," Elsie says with a smirk.

"Huh, that's funny. I had a similar dream, but I was winning." Mira chuckles. "Angelo is on his way to your room. He said you can join in after your session with Dr. Simone."

"Sounds good. Where are you off to? I want to visit each station. Can I go with you?"

"Sure, I'm just going to the room by the garden. My task is shucking peas and corn for the next few days, yay!" Mira says sarcastically.

They both head over to the preparation room. Only a few people are there, so Elsie finds a seat next to Mira. They chat and laugh for a couple of hours while shucking peas. Elsie almost forgets about her session.

"Oh, I need to get going!" She stands and whirls around, almost bumping into Mike. Her breath catches as she eyes him viciously, remembering what Hope told her.

"Well, who do we have here? I wasn't sure you were let out of your cave." Mike eyes her head to toe.

"Why don't you get out of here and leave her alone? No one wants trouble," Mira says, standing as if poised to leap at him.

"If no one wanted trouble, they would throw this bitch out." He leans toward Elsie. "I don't know how you got here or where you're from, but trust me, I will find a way to get you to talk."

"You're the last one I would talk to about anything. Just leave me alone. I won't bother you, you don't bother me," Elsie hisses, staring him down.

Mike turns on his heel and heads toward the barn. Elsie turns back to Mira.

"Are you okay?" Mira asks.

"I suppose running into him is going to be part of life here, so I have to get used to it. I'll be fine. See you later." Elsie waits an extra minute and then hurries through the garden, hoping not to run into Mike again.

At the session, Dr. Simone starts right up. "Okay, Elsie, let's try again. I think we were making progress yesterday, so let's see if we can dig a little deeper. Close your eyes and steady your breath." After a beat, she adds, "You seem a bit shaken up. Is everything alright?"

Elsie decides there's no reason to keep anything Mike does or says to her a secret. "Yes, I had another run-in with Mike the electrician. He came onto me a few days ago. It's okay, though. I want to get on with this." Elsie sits with her hands on her knees as she has done before.

"Okay, if you're sure."

Dr. Simone begins counting. As usual, Elsie closes her eyes and steadies her breathing. She thinks of the colors of the rainbow. *Red, orange, yellow, green, blue, indigo* . . . Elsie opens her eyes after the fifth repetition.

"I'm sorry. It's just hard to focus right now. I can do this," she sighs.

"Are you sure you want to do this so soon?" Dr. Simone holds Elsie's hands in hers.

"Yes. I need to find out who that guy was, what we were to each other." Elsie stares down at her feet, the memory of what she "saw" yesterday still stuck in her mind: Max on the ground, choking and gasping for air, as she watches him, powerless.

"Okay, close your eyes and take your time to focus. Count. Build your rainbow."

Elsie does as she is told and begins to build her rainbow.

Elsie is running down a hallway. She reaches a door marked 319 and pushes it open. She hears bricks smashing on the sidewalk outside, the building rocking beneath her feet. But she doesn't care. She has to get to her grandmother; she has to know if she is still alive.

Elsie doesn't find her in the living room or the kitchen. *Maybe she got out; maybe she's with friends or neighbors*, she thinks. Her hope dies swiftly. She finds her grandmother face down on the bed, struck by a hunk of concrete and rebar. It appears to have punched through the wall. Elsie can see right across the street through the hole. Elsie sinks next to the bed, sobbing. Her grandmother's eyes and mouth are open as though she was yelling for help with her last breath.

They're all gone—her mother, father, brother and sister, and now her grandmother too. She is alone.

She doesn't want to move even as the building shifts again. She hears shouting, but she doesn't care. She will stay here with her grandmother. Then they won't be alone; they will have each other.

Gradually, someone's shouts turn into words. "Anyone here?

Hello?" Suddenly she feels hands around her arms, lifting her up.

"The building's coming down. We gotta get out of here! Let's go!"

"No, I can't leave her! Let me go! I want to stay with her!" Elsie screams as he drags her from the apartment.

"You can't stay here. You can't help her! The whole thing is about to come down!"

Elsie sags to the floor, but the young man lifts her over his shoulder and jogs out of the building. He continues to run as the building tumbles down.

"No! No! Grandma!"

She sobs and screams until her throat is raw.

About a block and a half away from the rubble of the apartment building, the young man sets Elsie on the ground. She crouches down into a ball and sobs. Her rescuer watches her, clearly unsure what to do next. When Elsie finally looks up at him, she sees tears on his cheeks. He has short brown hair and kind eyes.

"Thank you for saving me. I wasn't going to leave." She stands to face him.

"It's fine. I'm glad I was there. My sister lived in that building, but she . . ." His voice chokes, and he shakes his head. "I just got back from a work trip to Florida and came back to all this." He motions widely with his arms. "I'm Max. Max Barton."

Elsie follows the direction of his gesture. She was so intent on getting to her family that she hasn't fully comprehended the magnitude of what has happened. The buildings still standing nearby are shells of what they once were, the concrete and stone blackened and all the windows blown out. The skyline, once marked by Fountain Place and Reunion Tower, is hidden behind smoke. Or maybe it is only smoke now. Her feet rest on a layer of glass and rubble.

Tears flow down her cheeks as she looks back at Max.

"Elsie Fitzgerald. My grandmother lived in that apartment building. My family is gone. I went to their house, and it was . . ."

Elsie can't finish.

"I understand. My parents, they're dead too. I don't know what to do now."

For a good five minutes, they stand in silence as the world crumbles around them.

"The only thing I can think of is to look for other survivors. There's strength in numbers, and maybe we can find a place to hunker down," Elsie says desperately.

"Does that mean I can travel with you?"

"I would like that very much. I wouldn't want to be alone. Though"—Elsie stares around at the devastation—"I don't think we're going to find much."

"Worth a try, right?" Max holds out his hand to her, and she takes it.

Dr. Simone regards Elsie with patient understanding as Elsie opens her eyes and struggles to find her words.

"It still doesn't feel real," she sighs, feeling like a broken record. "But the pain of losing my family and my grandmother, that feels real." She stares hard at the floor, willing the tears coating her cheeks to vanish.

"Even if it doesn't feel like a true memory, you still saw your grandmother; you still witnessed her death. It's okay to have that pain, Elsie."

"I need to know more. I need to figure out what happened to me. Can we try this again tomorrow?" Elsie begs.

"Of course. I'll be here," Dr. Simone assures her.

Elsie walks in a daze. She hears someone calling her name but ignores it. Walking to Mira's room, she stops at the table in the common area. Then she sits and begins sobbing.

Angelo enters the suite behind her.

"Elsie" is all he says. Elsie rises and steps into his arms, and he holds her as she lets her tears flow unimpeded. They stand in this position for what feels like an eternity.

"My mother," he finally says, clearing his throat. Elsie glances up. He's never spoken of his mother. "She started complaining of pain in her abdomen. We thought she was overworked. We thought maybe she just needed rest. The next day she couldn't get up. It took two weeks of her suffering and us trying any medications we had from our scavenge runs before she gave up. She said to me, 'Take care of them, *hijo*. Always take care of them.' Then she left us." He buries his face in Elsie's hair.

"I saw my grandmother. I saw her dead; she was alone. I was too late. I was too late for all of them. I should have been there. I should have died with them," Elsie sobs.

"Don't say that. You were spared for a reason. I don't know where you came from, but you're here now, and there has to be a reason for that. I'm sorry you're reliving these losses again. I really am."

Angelo leans back and looks into her eyes.

"But you are giving people here hope. I don't know how you do it, but after they talk to you, they seem inspired. They want to try new things and do more. You are here for a reason, and I really think eventually we will find out why."

Elsie wipes her face with the backs of both hands. "Thank you, Angelo. I appreciate that." She pauses and remembers where she is. "I'm sorry. You're busy, and I'm distracting you. I must look a mess."

"You look . . ." Angelo clears his throat. "You look fine. I'm going to go check on some things in the garden. I'll see you later."

When he leaves, Elsie remains rooted to the spot, wondering what to do. She wants to return to Dr. Simone and learn more—and she also wants to bury her memories forever.

She eventually wanders into Mira's room and lies on the mattress. Almost immediately, she hears footsteps at the opening.

"Want to talk about it?"

Mira settles on the floor next to the mattress.

"I saw it. I saw how I met Max. He carried me out of the building I found my grandmother in just as it was collapsing. She was dead.

I was crying and he pulled me out." She feels numb saying it now. "This man saved my life, and all I have left of him is these images in my mind. It's killing me."

Mira rubs Elsie's back. "I know in my soul that you are going to remember and everything is going to work out. Just trust the process and feel your feelings. It's okay." She pulls Elsie into a deep hug.

"I hope you're right, Mira. I feel so . . . burdened. I'm putting all this pressure on myself, and it's all amounting to nothing."

"Well, maybe that's the problem." Mira stops to think. "Maybe you need a good night's sleep and a morning off. Maybe throwing yourself into our little world isn't the best course for you. Maybe you need to just observe and absorb instead of forcing yourself to be a part of it."

"That isn't a bad idea," Elsie muses. "I think I will do that the next couple of days. Just take it all in. Watch everyone. That couldn't hurt, right?"

Mira smiles encouragingly. "And I think you should rest again for now. I can bring you food ag—"

"No. I mean, yes, I will rest for a bit here now, but I want to come out for dinner tonight. Get my mind off things."

"Okay." Mira hugs Elsie again and leaves her to rest.

* * *

When Elsie meets up with Dr. Simone the next morning, she is determined to work through whatever lurks in her memories.

"I want these memories to come back," she declares without so much as a "Good morning."

Dr. Simone looks momentarily taken aback, then amused.

"Are you sure you don't want to take a moment to talk through everything you've been remembering?"

"There's no point. It would be like talking about the plot of a book in school. Purely academic. That's why we have to keep going. We have to get to the bottom of everything!" Elsie tries to smile calmly to balance out her mania.

Dr. Simone leans forward. "Okay. Start building your rainbow, and I will start counting."

She approaches a cave opening. Angelo is standing there. She goes to him and asks what he's doing. He turns, regarding her intently as if trying to look into her soul. "I need to know what's in your mind, Elsie. What are you thinking?"

"That's easy." She rises on her tiptoes and kisses him. He returns the kiss. It is passionate and tender at the same time. He begins to kiss her neck, and she moans, "Oh, Angelo."

Elsie opens her eyes and stares in horror at Dr. Simone, who smiles without judgment or coyness.

"I brought you back. While those thoughts are worth exploring, that is not what we are trying to accomplish here, so I thought it best to have you redirect," she says. "I think you need more time before diving back in."

"I appreciate that. I honestly don't know what that was about," Elsie mutters.

"Elsie, I am not obligated to tell anyone anything unless it's dangerous to those here in the cavern," Dr. Simone reminds her.

Elsie eyes her. "What defines dangerous?"

"Let's say you were planning on blowing up the cavern or stabbing one of our members—things like that would qualify. What you just experienced in your mind is none of my business unless you want it to be."

"Well, what do you think it means? I mean, I don't have feelings for him," Elsie says, trying to sound convincing.

"I think it could mean anything. It could be that you sense his disapproval of your being here, so you will try any means to gain his trust," she explains.

"Like seduce him?! I am *not* planning on seducing him," Elsie laughs.

"Our minds work in mysterious ways, Elsie, and dreams like to cut through the nuance. It could merely be a representation of what you are feeling. For instance, this push to unearth your memories, perhaps to the detriment of your mental health, to assuage his doubts about you."

Elsie regards her thoughtfully for several moments.

"In order for us to move on with what we need to accomplish here, you need to resolve whatever issues you and Angelo are having so that those thoughts don't intrude in trying to recover your memories. Do you understand what I mean?" Dr. Simone asks.

"Yes, I understand. Though I don't know what I can do. I haven't been in a situation like this before."

"But I am sure you have had issues with people in the past? Or had strong feelings for them? And I'm sure you dealt with it then."

"Yes, but I was younger then. Stupid." Elsie shakes her head. "The stakes are higher now, if that makes sense."

"It absolutely does. So, you need to think about adult models from your past. How have they handled conflict in relationships? What type of relationship did you have with your family, or other classmates?"

"It hurts to think about them, so I've been trying not to," Elsie sighs. "My parents were great. They were married for thirty years. They were strict but fair. They used to let my sister, brother, and me get away with just enough before they finally put their foot down. My mother would cook huge meals on the weekend and feed everyone in the neighborhood. It was a free-for-all at our house."

Elsie tears up. "My sister and I would fight a lot, but makeups were quick. She was my best friend before I left for college. My brother was young, under ten years old when I went away. I miss him yelling at me for tickling him too much.

"I didn't have a lot of friends outside my sorority and a few classes. My roommate and a couple others I would go out to eat with from time to time. I kept to my studies and sorority functions. I was in a couple short relationships with boys, but nothing serious. So I guess I really don't know how to deal with this sort of thing."

"Communication is always key. Perhaps let Angelo know how you are feeling, regardless of what those feelings might be, and maybe you can move past whatever is blocking your memories from coming forth," Dr. Simone suggests.

"Okay, I will try. Thank you, Dr. Simone. Same time and place tomorrow."

Dr. Simone stands with Elsie and lightly touches her patient's shoulder. "Thank you for sharing with me."

Elsie takes a deep breath. *Now is as good a time as any to talk to Angelo.* She feels that maybe this truce between them is no longer a truce after last night, and maybe that is why she had that vision. Maybe she does want to resolve their relationship. The imagined kiss gave her goose bumps. If Angelo kissed her like that for real, would she feel it all over her body, like an electric shock?

Elsie shakes those thoughts from her head. Angelo is being nice to her now, but kissing her is probably the farthest thing from his mind. Therefore, it must be the farthest thing from hers.

Elsie reaches the cave and sees the men have gotten pretty far with the exposed wall, carving huge divots in it.

Angelo smiles as he turns to her. "How did your session go? You're back a little earlier; does that mean you remembered anything?"

Elsie shuts down. She stares into his eyes, remembering his kiss. She looks to his lips quickly and then looks down, frowning. She has freely volunteered every little detail of what she has learned in her sessions without prompting, and she resents that his first and last concern when it comes to her is when she will remember her past and get out of his hair.

"No. I promised you I would tell you if I did." She glares at him, suddenly recognizing him as the source of the burden on her shoulders. "Can we not talk about the session, for once?"

Angelo stops smiling and seems suspicious. "Okay, no problem, Elsie. We can let it go today."

"Thank you. It looks like you guys have made some progress," she comments, trying to push down her anger.

"Yes, it's coming along, but we still have a ways to go. We're going to call it a day now because we have to finish up our chores," Angelo answers icily.

"Of course. I'm going to find Andrea and the kids. Maybe that will take my mind off things." Elsie turns sharply and heads for the garden.

* * *

Her afternoon with Andrea and the children is quiet and just what Elsie needs to distract her. They walk back to the main cavern together and find Marco waiting at Andrea's home with a soccer ball.

"Hey, Tabby, Elton. Want to kick the ball around for a bit?" he asks, barely looking at Andrea. The children cheer and follow him to the back of the cave to play.

"Well, that was a little cold. How are the two of you doing?" Elsie asks.

"We're fine. He likes to focus on the kids when he's in soccer mode."

Mira approaches and invites them to play cards before dinner. Andrea retrieves toys for Zander's entertainment while Elsie joins Mira at a table.

Elsie is grateful to stop talking about her memories and simply be part of the group. She smiles as she looks around the cavern and sees everyone returning from their chores to settle in for dinner. She sees Angelo enter from the back and quickly turns her attention back to Mira. She can't keep avoiding him. She must resolve these feelings and thoughts. Her memories are too important to put on the back burner.

CHAPTER SEVEN

THE NEXT FEW days pass more leisurely. They all agree to take care of their chores in the mornings and work on the cave wall in the afternoon before dinner. Elsie takes the mornings to observe and take it easy.

Meanwhile, her sessions with Dr. Simone grow more intense.

"We don't have money. We have to walk. We can take breaks and eat what we can scavenge. We have no choice," Max says, shaking his head.

"I just don't understand what's going on. Each town we get to is practically deserted. It doesn't make sense." Elsie peers up an empty street. The bus ran out of gas, and the few people on it were forced to walk. Elsie and Max chose to head to the next town, about three square miles of one-story structures squatting on flat desert leading to mountains in the distance. The stores and restaurants have been looted, and there isn't anyone around.

They continue down the main street and notice a light on in a house down a side street. Approaching cautiously, they climb rickety steps to a wraparound porch and knock on the front door. An elderly lady answers abruptly, swinging the door open with a shovel raised above her shoulders.

"What the hell do you want? Leave me alone!" she shouts.

Max raises his hands. "Whoa, we mean no harm. We just walked into this town from a broken-down bus and wondered where everyone was."

Elsie inches in front of him. "We won't hurt anyone. We're traveling from Dallas. What town is this? Where is everyone?"

The woman squints at Elsie and lowers her shovel but doesn't put it down.

"This is Van Horn. With the war, no supplies have been coming in, and everyone went berserk. They started stealing stuff and attacking each other. Some people were having breathing problems, so they just stayed in their homes. Like I'm trying to do," she says meaningfully.

"We don't want to disturb you. Can we just have some water?" Elsie asks in as subdued a manner as she can muster.

The woman steps back from the door. "Come in and I'll give you a little something to eat and drink. But that's all!" Max and Elsie look at each other and nod gratefully, thanking the woman before entering her home. They enter a family room furnished with a couch, love seat, and reclining chair. A battery-operated radio sits on a TV table next to the recliner. Off the family room is a small hallway with a bedroom on one side and a bathroom on the other. The hallway leads directly back to the kitchen.

"Have a seat on the couch. Don't think about taking anything. I don't have anything of value anyway. I'll get you some water, and I think I have some bread to spare." She shuffles to the kitchen. Max and Elsie lower cautiously onto the love seat together with their hands on their knees. They are afraid to move or do anything that might set off the woman. She returns with two glasses of cloudy water and two slices of white bread.

"Name's Rhonda. I make my own bread, but soon I'll be out of those ingredients, so enjoy it while you can."

"Thank you so much, Rhonda. We really appreciate it," Elsie says as she accepts the glasses and the bread. She hands one of each to Max.

"So, you came from Dallas, huh? Lucky you survived that hot mess."

"We weren't there when the bombs hit. We were both away and came back to see if our families survived," Max explains.

"They didn't," Elsie says softly, meeting Rhonda's eyes so she can see they are merely lost and afraid.

"I am sorry to hear that. Listen, you seem like good kids. You can stay the night here. Get a good night's sleep, and then head out again in the morning. I don't have provisions to take on house guests permanently, but it's okay for one night. Don't think of trying anything, though. I have a shotgun by my bed, and if I hear anything out of place, I will use it." With that, she leans back in the recliner and turns on the radio.

"Thank you so much. We really appreciate it. We promise we won't be a problem at all," Max says. Rhonda hushes him and turns up the radio.

On the news, the announcer is talking about more bombings throughout the country and in smaller cities, causing panic and chaos. He reports that people are dying from respiratory issues. They suspect some of the bombs may have carried a bioagent. The news is terrifying.

"What if no place is safe?" she whispers to Max. "What if there's nothing left?"

"Then we go to the mountains and live there if we have to. We'll make it somehow, Elsie, I promise," Max says with an expression of sheer determination.

They both sleep in the family room that night. Elsie takes the love seat and Max the couch. They sleep as well as they could hope for despite the news. In the morning, Rhonda gives them both bottles filled with water and two slices of bread each.

"This is too much, Rhonda. You have to keep some for yourself," Elsie protests.

Rhonda gives her a wry look. "I am an old lady. Who knows how long I have? I'm rooting for you both. If I can help even a little, well, maybe I will get into heaven." She smiles. They thank her and are on their way.

They stop at a store on the way out of town. It has been thoroughly ransacked, but some backpacks and clothing remain. They change clothes and fill the backpacks with other clothing, hoping no one will stop them. Then they continue down the highway, which is just as empty as the town they left.

Elsie opens her eyes and focuses on Dr. Simone. She reaches for some emotion to connect to Max. "I don't think we were a couple. I mean romantically. I feel like we were just two people trying to survive together. But this is so frustrating! This isn't helping me remember how I got here."

"I don't know if that's true. You *are* remembering. I am sure with more time and more pieces, we can connect the dots and figure out how you got here."

"It doesn't seem fair to Max. We were each other's company in a world that was falling apart, and I can't even remember him properly," Elsie says, staring at a spot on the table.

"Perhaps you can meditate on these memories. Remember them as you saw them, and maybe something will click," Dr. Simone offers.

"I suppose. Have you ever heard of anyone forgetting their life the way I have?" Elsie asks.

Dr. Simone rises and circles the table to sit next to Elsie. "Yes. People with PTSD tend to build a wall around traumatic memories, and it takes a lot to break that wall. Your wall is transparent, in a way. You see the memory, but your body is protecting you from the heartache and pain you felt. Yet it's still just a matter of breaking that wall."

"Well, I don't know if that makes me feel better, but at least, to your point, I am remembering things. Thank you, Dr. Simone. I really appreciate all the help you're giving me."

At that moment, Angelo and Mira venture over to the table.

"Hi. We figured we would come over and see if Elsie was done for the day," Mira says.

"Yes, we're finished here. Elsie is doing a great job. We are progressing slowly but surely." Dr. Simone looks at Angelo as she speaks, as though giving a report.

"That is good to hear. We were going to take a walk in the garden and check on things. Did you want to join us?" Angelo asks Elsie.

"Sure, my brain is fried." Elsie stands and joins Mira and Angelo. "See you later, Dr. Simone."

As the three enter the tunnel, Elsie asks, "What's prompting this walkabout?"

"We got done with our chores a little early today and wanted to take in the scenery, is all. We thought you might want to join us," Angelo says.

Mira walks slightly ahead of Elsie and Angelo. If Elsie were to guess, Mira wants Angelo and Elsie to talk to each other. With that directive, Elsie smiles at Angelo.

"I am still in awe that you were a golfer."

"I only fooled around with it with friends. My father enjoyed it and taught me how to play when I was younger," he says.

"You haven't mentioned him. Where was he when all this happened?" Elsie asks as they reach the garden.

"He had asthma. He had an attack at work a year before all this happened and he couldn't come back from it. When the bombs first hit, he went downhill fast. He died in the hospital."

"I am so sorry. That's awful."

"We were able to say goodbye. It was hardest on my mom, but at least we were together," Mira adds as she drops back to join them.

"I owe my dad a lot," Angelo says. "He was a strict man and didn't let us get away with much, but when he had time available, he spent it with us. He worked as a contractor and taught me everything he knew. I don't think I would be the man I am today if he hadn't helped me become one."

"I'm glad you got to say goodbye to both your parents. It really sucks you had to say it at all, but it is a true blessing."

Mira pulls her in for a side hug.

"I'm sorry you didn't get to say goodbye to your family, Elsie," Angelo says.

"To be fair, we assume I didn't, but maybe that was the traumatic event that started this all. Maybe I did say goodbye and then the next five years were a blur until, well, I don't know when the exact moment was that I decided to forget it all."

Elsie stares ahead, lost in thought. She then looks down to behold a patch of purple flowers. For a moment, she is disoriented.

"These flowers, these purple ones in the middle here—these are what I was eating in my memory with Max. What are these called?" She touches one, her hand shaking.

"It says here it is an *Astragalus* plant. I've never really paid attention to the flowers, so I don't know how common they are or where they grew," Angelo says, crouching to read the label on the flower patch.

"Why can't they just have easy names like 'purple panther flower'?" Elsie asks.

Mira looks closer at the flower. "I think I've read about these plants. They help with strengthening the immune system and with respiratory illnesses. People would take extract from the root and use it in teas and such."

"Well, that sounds like a handy plant to have around. Let's get back so we can start working on the cave," Angelo says, sounding restless.

Elsie lingers and stares at the pretty purple flower that she feels fed not only her body but her soul. *Why am I drawn to this plant?* She must have been starving to have eaten these. Mira pulls her from her trance.

"Hey, are you coming?"

"Yeah, I just . . . They really are beautiful, huh?"

Mira smiles back and sighs, glancing back at the flowers as they move on. "They do add some beauty to this dark life we're living." They laugh and link arms, walking back to the cave entrance together.

* * *

A few days later, Elsie wakes and dresses in her Keep Calm tee and new jeans. When she comes to the common area, she spots a mug with a few sprigs of the *Astragalus* flowers. She smiles when she finds a note under the mug.

Good morning, Elsie. This is the chore rotation schedule for the week. Marjorie put it together, and I was able to get it from her before she posted it. You are in the water filtration room with Hope. I hope you like the flowers.
Angelo

Elsie plucks up one of the flowers and brings it to her nose. It's not overly fragrant, but the smell of a flower always makes her cheerful.

"And who, might I ask, gave you those?" Mira comes in, smiling knowingly.

"I think you have a clue. It is a very nice gesture for one friend to give another flowers," Elsie says haughtily as Marco wanders in. "Right, Marco? I am sure you give Andrea flowers sometimes."

"I have in the past, and we are most definitely friends," he sighs heavily. "Those are very pretty. Maybe if I had given her those, she would look at me as a little more than that."

Mira laughs and rubs Marco's head, mussing his hair. "Doubtful.

You're just always going to be cute little Marco!"

"Stop it! You know I hate that!" he yells.

"Well, we better get to our chores. I'm on shucking and shelling duty again, and Lord knows how much I love that," Mira says.

"I can't wait to start mine! I know you guys are probably bored to death of your chores but this is my first time, so I am excited," Elsie says as she grabs a protein bar from the shelf and heads out the door. She spots Hope strolling toward the opening and hurries to catch up.

"Good morning, Hope! We're doing water filtration together."

"Excellent. Have you done it before?"

"No, I've observed a little but haven't actually done it."

"Well, I'll show you how it's done, and we'll get to it." Hope says perkily. "First we have to collect all the morning water bins and dump them into the barrel by the door."

They spend the morning collecting water and bringing it to the barrels, then using a wagon to bring the full barrels to the filter contraption close to the waterwheel.

"We dump the water through here, where it starts to filter and then it is further filtered by the wheel. The water then goes through a secondary underwater filter and fills the lake, where we get all the clean water for ourselves and the plants. After we do all this, we have to collect the water used for cleaning the fruits and vegetables, as well as what drips under the plants after watering," Hope explains.

Elsie is still amazed at how well developed this entire system is. After they finish collecting the water from the garden and cleaning room, they journey to the waste room to collect the urine and start the process again.

"Okay, this is my least favorite part of this," Elsie says with a laugh.

"Could be worse; you could be making fertilizer right now," Hope giggles in response. As they're dumping the waste into the water filter, Mike enters from the living quarters Elsie explored her first week there. He stares at the women as he walks through but doesn't say one word. Both women stare back until he's gone.

"God, he is the creepiest guy ever," Hope says. "Has he talked to you again?"

"We had an encounter, but it was brief. Hopefully I won't have to deal with him again."

"Better you than me." Her eyes widen and she adds, "Because you are a lot tougher than I am."

"Not tougher. I just have the knowledge to defend myself. I took self-defense in school. I can show you sometime if you want."

"That would be awesome. Even if I never use it, it would be good exercise!" Hope looks nervous. "I don't ever want to get myself in that situation again."

"I just hope he's the only asshole around here," Elsie states frankly.

"I didn't even think of that."

"We just need to stick together and never leave each other alone with anyone we aren't one hundred percent sure of. That will be your first lesson in self-defense," Elsie says with a smile.

"A good lesson, and great plan."

When they finish for the day, Hope says, "We can head to the main cavern for lunch. I think Jeremy made bread today to have with soup!"

They return to the main cavern and serve themselves lunch, chatting about life before the cavern. Hope was accepted to Boston University, among other colleges, and was contemplating living in a big city.

Elsie finds everyone's former plans and dreams fascinating. They're devastating too, though. Everyone here has lost so much, not just people but opportunities. She explains as much to Dr. Simone during her session.

"It is a lot to take in, when you think of the number of people here," Dr. Simone agrees.

"It's overwhelming."

"Well, hold on to that feeling. Maybe you can use it to reach into your mind. Let's begin, shall we?" Dr. Simone encourages. "I am going to count, and you build your rainbow. One, two, three..."

Elsie builds her rainbow about four times before a memory comes forward.

She is in a white room that looks like a hospital room. It has a hospital bed and a nightstand. There is a closet across from the bed, and Elsie is returning from the closet with a book. She perches on the bed with her legs crisscrossed.

A woman enters, the same woman from her previous memory: Lily. Lily sits across from Elsie on the bed.

"Hello, Elsie, can I visit for a bit?"

"Of course! I look forward to our talks. It's the one thing that helps pass the time. I'm still dying to know how you weren't fired for smacking that director on the set of *Mysteries and Lies*," Elsie says.

"Well, the producer gave me a stern talking-to, but they knew they wouldn't sell tickets to that movie without me, so they needed me. They told me, though, that they would rewrite my contract if I pulled that crap again," she says with a warm smile.

"Well, I guess no one can get away with everything."

"Which is one of the things that brings me here today. Nothing concrete is coming from your blood. Charles would like a biopsy of your lung, but I fear that is too invasive."

"It's fine."

"Elsie, I don't think you understand." Lily places her hand over Elsie's.

"I do understand. I've been outside numerous times, and it is always the same thing. Others start choking and I don't. We have to find out why—how. It is important for our civilization, and I want to do my part. It is fine, Lily. I promise."

Elsie snaps back from this memory. It is the first memory she viscerally feels. She isn't just "watching" herself.

"That felt different. Like, I *felt* it. I wonder who that woman was. Do you think she's an Elite?" She smiles giddily. "I remember! I can't believe this!"

"This is wonderful, Elsie, but do you realize what it is you remember? You said that you could breathe outside. Do you think that was true?"

"It must be, right?" Elsie shakes her head in amazement.

"I think we need to get Angelo and the other leaders and tell them what we discovered today," Dr. Simone says firmly. "I think this is important."

"They're probably in my cave, trying to break through the wall. If you can find Marjorie, I'll meet you back here."

"Agreed." Dr. Simone heads for the gardens while Elsie hurries to her cave.

The men are where she suspected, all beating on the concrete wall.

"Hey, guys. Looks like things are coming along nicely here."

"Hey, Elsie. Yeah, it's slow and steady, but it's something. How did your session go?" Angelo wipes his forehead with his sleeve.

"That's what I came here to tell you. Carlos, Angelo, can you guys come to the far table with me? Sorry, Marco, I think it should be discussed with the leaders first."

"Hey, that's fine with me. I'll stay here and hit on my date. My date being the wall. Get it? Hit on my date?"

"You are too young for Dad jokes, Marco. Leave that to the professionals," Carlos laughs.

Elsie leads Angelo and Carlos to the tables, where Dr. Simone and Marjorie are waiting.

"So, we've had a breakthrough that we feel should be discussed with you all," Dr. Simone says, motioning to Elsie.

"I had a real, honest-to-goodness memory of an encounter with someone in a hospital room. I don't remember why I was in a hospital room or when it occurred, but I do remember the conversation."

"Elsie, that is fantastic!" Angelo smiles. "I knew it was a matter of time."

"Well, that isn't all. In this conversation, I spoke with this woman about doing tests on me because, according to her, I can breathe the air. Everyone else chokes, but I don't. That would explain how I was outside and somehow wandered in here."

She watches doubt wash over the group.

"Elsie, what you are describing isn't possible," Carlos says. "Maybe this is something that took place when the air began going bad? I highly doubt you would be able to breathe out there now."

"There is one way to find out," Elsie retorts, realizing she shouldn't be surprised at their reaction.

Angelo begins to pace. "No. Absolutely not. There is no way I am letting you out. I am not risking you in the name of science."

"There is no need for it, Elsie," Marjorie explains for the group. "Even if you could breathe, no one else can. Knowing if you can or not is not helpful to any of us."

"But maybe—"

"No." Angelo halts. "I am happy for you, Elsie. However, Marjorie is right. There is no reason to test this theory out on you or anyone else. I will not risk anyone in this cavern on a what-if. For all we know, this memory of yours could be a dream."

"It doesn't feel that way, Angelo! I know this is real. I remember it!"

"But you don't remember when it took place or where. We do not have enough information to move forward. Maybe after more sessions with Dr. Simone, we can revisit. But right now, it is a hard no. Is everyone in agreement?"

Even Dr. Simone nods with the others. "We don't want to jump the gun, Elsie. We need a few more sessions of actual memories. Then we all can decide the best course of action."

This doesn't make Elsie feel any better.

"Okay. I'll respect your decision, but I feel in my heart that this is true."

"And you may be right, Elsie, but we don't have enough information to risk anyone's life." Carlos states as he gets up. "I'm going back to help Marco." Dr. Simone and Marjorie also depart, leaving Angelo and Elsie.

"Carlos is right. We can't compromise anyone's safety based on this one—"

Elsie interrupts him.

"Compromise with me! I'll go out for an hour!"

"No!" Angelo shouts. "You have become a part of this cavern, a part of this family! We will not compromise you either! Let it go!"

From the back of the cavern, hollers erupt, and they both immediately drop the subject, hurrying to Elsie's cave to find Marco and Carlos have broken through the cement wall. It is a small opening but an opening nonetheless.

"Looks like we're getting somewhere now!" Angelo cheers with a clap.

"Wow," Elsie says admiringly. "Why don't I get water so we have something to drink as we push through?"

Angelo crouches and peers through the wall. "That's a great idea. Thanks, Elsie," he says absently. Then he grabs a mallet and hits the concrete with such force that a new crack spiders horizontally from the hole.

Elsie sighs and ventures to the grand meeting room, where she finds a wagon, an empty pitcher, and a couple of empty water barrels by a table. Loading the barrels into the wagon, she trundles to the water filtration room.

There she fills pitcher after pitcher to fill the barrels. Distracted by her thoughts about her memory and everyone's reaction to it, she doesn't realize someone has entered the room until she hears her name.

Elsie turns quickly but doesn't have time to react before she's disoriented by a hard slap to the face. She stumbles back and falls, and Mike leaps on her, binding her legs with his and pinning her arms down.

"That was for kneeing me in the groin, you little bitch," he spits. "Now I'm going to get the truth from you, but maybe a little something extra first!" He presses his lips forcefully to hers. She tries to scream, but he sticks his tongue in her mouth, then pulls back and yanks her arms above her head with one hand, fumbling at her pants with the other. She sees with horror that his pants are already unbuttoned. As he stuffs a handkerchief into her mouth, he says, "That's a good girl. Just lay there and let me take you. You know you want it. You know you do." Crying now, Elsie strains to free herself. "I knew you would know how to mo—"

Then he vanishes, along with his weight on her, and she hears a breath-rattling thud. Sitting up in a panic, she sees Mike on his back, feet away. He tries to sit up. "What—"

The man who saved Elsie punches him in the jaw, and Mike slumps, unconscious. Elsie's rescuer turns and then glances aside as she pulls her pants back up around her hips.

"Are you alright?" he asks with a slight Southern accent. He's tan, with dark hair and dark eyes. There is a roughness about him, but his manner with her is gentle. Elsie recognizes the man but doesn't know his name.

"Yes, thank you for coming when you did. Another minute and, well . . ." Elsie locks down, then glances back up when he offers his hand.

"I was in the garden when Bart pulled me aside. He told me that Mike was up to no good with a young woman in this room. He said he didn't want to be the one to get involved, but he knew it was wrong and someone should help her out," the man explains.

"Are you Brian? Simone's husband?" Elsie asks, realization dawning. He used to be a police officer, she remembers.

"Yes, Miss Elsie. Simone speaks of you highly. I'm only sorry I didn't get here sooner. I'll make sure Angelo and the other leaders know what this scumbag tried to do."

He gives Mike a sharp kick in the ribs. Mike groans and wakes up.

"If you don't want me to knock your goddamned teeth out,

I suggest you get out of here until we figure out what the hell to do with you, asshole!" Brian snaps. Mike rolls over, muttering something incomprehensible, and gets up. He glances at Elsie and lurches out of the room.

"Thank you so much for your help, Brian," Elsie says shakily. She wants to vomit at what has to be done. She should be shouting about what Mike did to the rooftops. "However, as much as I want that man to pay for what he did, he's the head electrician, an essential worker. We can't lose him." She hates how dependent they all are on people they know nothing about. "I . . . I'll make sure that I don't go anywhere alone moving forward. Does that make sense?"

"I'm not sure that is the best solution, nor do I agree with it, but I will honor your wishes. If you need an escort at any time, Miss Elsie, I will be happy to be that escort for you," he insists.

"Thank you, Brian. And it's just Elsie." She looks him in the eye. "I truly appreciate you saving me and keeping it quiet. I am just going to wash my face really quick and then finish filling these barrels. They've broken through the wall, and I'm anxious to see what's behind there. And to just . . . put this behind me." She swallows hard.

Brian says, "I'll help with the barrels, Miss Elsie—I mean, Elsie. You do what you need to do to collect yourself."

Elsie takes deep breaths and flexes her hands, then walks to the edge of the lake, kneels, and washes her face. She can't help but cry some more. She needs to get it all out before going back. Brian continues to fill the barrels, not interrupting her at all. She washes her face again, stands, and shakes out her arms and legs.

"The barrels are filled. I hope it's alright if I wheel the wagon back to the cave. With you walking with me, of course, but I feel like you need to just concern yourself with you," Brian offers.

Her tears this time come from gratitude. "Thank you so much, Brian."

They walk back to the cave in silence. Elsie tries to concoct an excuse for taking so long, but Brian saves her from that as soon as they arrive.

"Brian," Angelo says with a note of surprise.

"I saw Miss Elsie with the wagon and barrels and asked if I could help. We got to talking, and she is such a pleasant young lady, we lost track of time. I insisted I help her bring back the water," Brain explains.

"Thank you, Brian." Angelo eyes Elsie a bit suspiciously. "Are you okay, Elsie? You look shaken."

"I'm fine," Elsie says, stiffening to hide the shaking.

"Okay." Angelo doesn't sound convinced. He takes a cup of water and hands it to Marco. "We got a little further, but we're calling it a day now to get ready for dinner. I'm going to talk to Carlos and Marjorie about a plan for when we get through. I think we may make a larger opening within the next day or two. When we do get through, we don't want everyone bombarding the entrance."

"Sounds like a good idea. I'll take this wagon back by the tables so it's ready for dinner." Elsie doesn't wait for anyone to respond, performing the task with haste before hurrying back to Mira's room to further gather herself. She knows what she went through is traumatic and she needs time to adjust. She knows she should probably tell someone what happened, but she doesn't trust Mike not to retaliate in some sinister way if she talks. This might not be the best decision, but these are not the best circumstances.

She remembers what Hope told her. Perhaps she can share with Hope what happened and together they can decide. She is ashamed at how quickly she let her guard down after their agreement to never go anywhere alone. However, she will definitely make it her job to ensure no woman in this cavern goes anywhere unescorted from now on.

Elsie makes her way to dinner. When she arrives at the tables, everyone is seated, with Angelo, Carlos, and Marjorie standing in front of the room beside the food. She sits next to Andrea and the children. Angelo clears his throat, and the room goes quiet.

"It looks as though we may break through the wall within the next few days. We've already made a hole, and the rest should give way a little easier. We will notify everyone once we break through. However, we cannot all be the first to see whatever is on the other side. Marjorie, Carlos, and I will go in along with Marco and Brian, just in case there is danger and we need some muscle. Everyone else will pull numbers from a hat. We will have groups of fifteen. You will receive a number between one and three. That will be your group. *If* it is safe and we feel it is worth everyone checking out, that is the order you will enter. If you do not wish to go, do not take a number. Each group will be escorted by one of us. We feel this is the fairest way for everyone to be a part of it. Does everyone agree to these terms?"

The assembled cave denizens nod eagerly.

Marjorie weaves around the room, carrying a hat filled with slips of papers. When she comes to Elsie's table, each occupant takes a number. By a stroke of luck, Elsie and Andrea are both in group one. Elsie scampers off to find Mira and learns that Mira and Amanda are as well.

"It's only fair that you should go in the first group since it was your room to begin with," Mira says as Elsie sits next to her. Angelo joins them at the table.

"I agree, but we didn't want to single you out, Elsie," he says.

"But if it's nothing but the back end of another room or something, I lose my room," Elsie laughs. Dr. Simone appears by Elsie's shoulder and greets the table.

"What number did you get?" Mira asks her.

"Number two. This way I can see for myself in case anyone needs to talk about it. Elsie, can I speak with you alone for a moment?"

"Sure." Elsie rises from the table. She has a funny feeling she knows what this is in regard to. They get to the far side of the cavern, away from everyone, who are all busily sharing their numbers and trying to guess what they might find.

"I spoke with Brian before dinner," Dr. Simone begins. "He told me what happened. I hope you're not angry with him for telling me, but from what he described, I think it was important he did."

"It's fine. I understand why he would tell you. I do trust you and trust you won't tell anyone. I am fine, though, really. Brian got there just in time, before any real damage was done," Elsie tells her, though she doesn't sound convincing even to herself.

"It doesn't matter how far he got, Elsie. Damage was still done. He had no right to put his hands on you."

"I know, and believe me, if circumstances were different, I would do everything in my power to make sure he saw some type of justice. But I understand how essential electricians are to our survival in these caverns. I don't trust him not to retaliate in some way if we go after him."

"You wouldn't be left alone, so he wouldn't be able to do anything to you in the future. You wouldn't have to worry about retaliation," Dr. Simone encourages.

"I'm not talking about me. I think he is a disgusting excuse for a human being, and I wouldn't put it past him to do something detrimental to everyone," Elsie says heatedly.

"I see. Well, I know you say you are fine, but I can't see how you would be. What he did was monstrous."

"I agree. He is a monster. Alright, I am shaken. It will take time, but I think this thing with the wall will take my mind off it. I just won't go anywhere alone."

"That is a must. If you want to talk about it, I'm here for you. It doesn't have to be limited to our sessions." Dr. Simone gives Elsie a hug, and Elsie hugs her back tight. The one good thing to come out of the end of the world is the sense of community and family Elsie has felt since coming here.

"Is everything okay?" Angelo asks, approaching slowly. "I don't want to interrupt, but I was getting a little nervous. Are you okay, Elsie?"

"Yes, still feeling the aftereffects of my recent memory is all," Elsie explains quickly.

"Okay, I understand. I'm going to retire for the night. Have a good one, ladies."

Angelo turns and heads for his room.

"I better get back before anyone else gets suspicious." Elsie rolls her eyes.

"If they don't break through the wall by the time of our session tomorrow, I'll see you then. If they do, I think we will all be too distracted to do anything else. However, if whatever we find behind that wall sparks memories or you want to talk about anything at all, please come find me immediately." Dr. Simone takes Elsie's hand.

"I promise, I will," Elsie says.

Elsie returns to the table, where Andrea has joined Mira and Amanda. Marco is off playing ball with the children.

"I've had a long day today. I think I might sneak off to bed," Elsie tells the group.

"I want to get my beauty sleep too. I want to make sure I have enough energy to investigate!" Mira declares, standing to walk with Elsie.

Elsie wishes for more dreams of Max no matter how depressing they may be. Anything is better than reliving her experience today with Mike. She hopes those images don't haunt her.

"So, I can tell something is up tonight. What is it?" Mira asks when they're alone in the room.

"Well, I had a memory today that was actually a memory. As in I remember the conversation," Elsie explains.

"Oh my God, Elsie! That is fantastic! What was it of?" Mira asks excitedly. Elsie tells Mira about the memory, and about telling the leaders about it.

"What do they think?"

"They want to sit on it for a bit. We don't know how valid it is since I can't remember the when or where."

"You remember it! How can it not be?"

"I know! That's why I volunteered to go out and test it."

"Okay, wait, now I get why they want to sit on it. No one is going to experiment with you going out there. That is just crazy talk."

"Not you too," Elsie sighs. Mira puts her hands on both of Elsie's shoulders and looks at her sternly.

"Promise me that you won't go out there. Please."

Elsie rolls her eyes. "I promise. I'm gutsy, but I am not completely stupid. I wouldn't go out by myself without backup." Not yet anyway.

"Good, now I can sleep well."

CHAPTER EIGHT

ELSIE WAKES TO a buzz in the air. Everyone is eager to see behind the wall. Elsie laughs at the thought that it might end up being something entirely mundane, like a forgotten utility room. What a letdown. But there has been so little to get excited about in the last five years. Whatever is behind that wall, the mystery is brightening eyes and giving everyone a reason to smile.

Elsie didn't sleep very well, but she did sleep. Afraid of her dreams, she kept shifting, from her side to her stomach and back, anything other than the position that asshole held her down in. Finally, she fell asleep. Perhaps luckily, by morning, any dreams have disappeared from her memory like the past five years.

Elsie arrives at her room and finds a small crowd. She hears smashing and sounds of breaking concrete. It seems Angelo, Carlos, and Marco have wasted no time again today. Angelo steps out, and everyone holds their breath.

"Good morning, everyone. We still have a way to go with the wall. I ask everyone in groups two and three to get your chores over with so you can come back and check our progress later. Group one will wait here and carry out the concrete and dirt that we remove. After group one has your turn, it will be important that you complete your chores for the day so the other groups can have their turns. We must work together to make sure this goes smoothly."

Brian arrives with a wagon of water barrels. He nods at Elsie. Elsie shivers at the sight of the wagon but refuses to let that deter her from the task at hand.

The crowd begins to thin out. The members of groups two and three express disappointment at missing the initial excitement but understand why they need to go. Meanwhile, Mira organizes an assembly line. Amanda makes sure she is closest to the front. Elsie takes a spot between Marjorie and Hope.

"Okay, they will break the concrete and fill these baskets. We'll pass them down the line to be dumped in the far corner, where it has been going. Does everyone understand?" Mira announces.

"Isn't this exciting? I hope something good is there," Hope says.

Elsie smiles back, remembering that she still needs to tell Hope what happened with Mike.

Andrea arrives with her children and waves to Elsie, taking her place at the end of the line and explaining to the children that they have the important job of running the cement buckets to the corner. They all look extremely serious and invested in their task. The first bucket comes along. Then another.

This goes on for an hour or so before the men begin to shout.

Elsie hears Angelo say, "Brian, why don't you go in first while we continue to make the opening a little larger. Take the flashlight."

Everyone starts grinning and bouncing. The moment has arrived! Angelo and Brian are talking, but Elsie can't make out any words over the banging and smashing. The noise stops.

"What the hell?" Angelo exclaims. "Is there a light, Brian? See if you can find a switch. I'll be right behind you."

It is quiet for a few moments, and then Angelo emerges from the entrance.

"It's a room. It looks like a supply room. We ask that everyone enter one at a time; please don't push or shove. We found a light switch, so there is plenty of light. Please don't touch anything that looks dangerous or suspicious."

He turns to enter, and the rest follow slowly. Elsie ducks in and walks into an all-white room, apparently built with drywall and cement. Above them hang flickering fluorescent lights. Large metal cabinets and shelves line the walls. In the center is a line of six large metal boxes, about waist height.

Once everyone is inside, Angelo announces, "I would like everyone to take a corner or side of the room and start looking inside these cabinets. Again, please don't touch anything suspicious."

Elsie and Mira go immediately to a set of cabinets that have a clear glass front. Mira opens the door to one and removes small, labeled glass bottles. She looks in the cabinet below it and finds bandages and bottles.

"This is a medical storage unit. These are antibiotics and medications that have been frozen. I didn't know that was even possible. There are first aid supplies down here. Hydrogen peroxide, alcohol, gauze; it's all here." Mira looks mystified.

Suddenly Hope cries out from the center of the room, where she has opened the metal boxes to reveal that they are chest freezers.

"Oh my God! There's meat in here! These are freezers with chicken, steak, and pork, I think. They've been vacuum-sealed and frozen! There are so many in here!"

Amanda shouts from another corner of the room, "Angelo!" From a set of plain white cabinets she pulls out a box of chocolate sandwich cookies with a delighted grin and immediately opens the box, taking one to eat. "Angelo, have one! They aren't stale or anything!"

"Amanda, I don't think you should eat anything from here. We don't know what this is or what it's for," Angelo scolds her. Brian and Carlos investigate the cabinets Amanda is rummaging through.

"It looks like it's running on some kind of vacuum system," Carlos says. He closes the door and presses a button on the side. They hear a sucking sound. "That's how they keep everything from going stale. I wonder who came up with this system; it's brilliant."

He opens it again. "There is pasta and sauces in here, snacks, tea and coffee."

"Look at this!" Marjorie says. "There are clothes in here! Dresses, suits, blouses, pants, and skirts, even some shoes." She holds a sparkling gown up against her body with a giggle. "Maybe we can have that party Elsie was talking about!"

"What is this place? It has to have been here since the cavern was created, right?" Marco asks the group.

"It seems to be a supply locker of some sort. I wonder how many more of these they have. I can't imagine they would only have this one if there are still so many supplies in here after five years," Marjorie says. Elsie wanders the room. She still can't believe her eyes.

"Okay, everyone. Let's take this slow. I can't believe the Elite would just forget about this room," Angelo warns.

"Finders keepers, that's for damn sure. They have been holding out on us," Amanda says, shoving another cookie in her mouth.

"Okay, no one eat or touch anything else. We will allow the other groups to have their turns in here. After that, Marjorie, Carlos, Mira, and I will take inventory. We will make sure that we ration—"

"*Ice cream*!" Hope hollers. "They have ice cream in here! Every major flavor you can think of: chocolate, vanilla, butter pecan, mint chocolate chip. They even have those drumstick cone things in here!" Hope is pulling out gallons of ice cream and holding them up for everyone to see.

"Okay, okay. I know it looks like we will have the chance to indulge a bit, but before we take anything out, and I do mean anything, *Amanda*"—Angelo looks to Amanda, who puts down the cookies she was clutching protectively—"we have to find out exactly what is in here and why. If it is a supply room, we have to know why it's still here and if there's a plan for it before we ransack it."

"I think we should assign someone to watch over the room. Have a sign-out sheet of what they want to take out once you have the inventory done," Mira says, still sorting through all the medical supplies, completely ignoring what Angelo is saying.

"I like the idea of a party. We don't need to have everything all at once, but it would be nice to celebrate, don't you all think?" Andrea offers, after taking in the room.

"That sounds like a great idea. First, we take inventory. Next we plan a party to use *some* of the fun stuff that is in here. The clothing, the snacks, and a steak dinner to boot!" Marco smiles.

"Then whatever is left we either ration or have a sign-out sheet. I think that sounds fair," Mira finishes.

Angelo shakes his head. "Let's think about this first. I agree we should first take inventory. We are certainly not going to use the food we found tonight for dinner. Let's take a day, at least, before we start taking anything out. We need to process. I do like Mira's idea about a sign-out sheet, but we can't just start stealing from the people who have taken care of us for five years without asking ourselves a few key questions. Why is this room still packed full of supplies? What is on the other side of that door?"

As one, the group swings to look at the very obvious door on the side of the room opposite the hole they created.

"And is anyone going to come in at any point?" Angelo finishes firmly. The others edge back from the door at that, and Elsie shakes her head, amazed at how blind excitement made her.

"Do you see how brand-new, shiny, and unsmudged everything in here is?" Mira then asks. "No doubt they've got dozens of these storerooms, and with us constantly providing them food, who's to say they'll ever get to this room?"

Angelo eventually agrees—very reluctantly—to risk angering their benefactors for the sake of morale, and survival. After all, the medicines alone could be lifesaving.

"At dinner, we'll put the idea of a party to a vote," he finishes.

Angelo asks the other leaders and his siblings to stay back so that they can show the others what is in each area. The rest of the group exits. Angelo goes to Elsie and pulls her back lightly. "You're awfully quiet, Elsie. Is everything okay?"

"Yes, of course. I'm just in awe like everyone else. It is a nice surprise, right?" Elsie turns from him, not expecting an answer.

Back out in front of the cave, they find a small group waiting.

"What is it? Is there anything of use to us?" the others clamor. Andrea explains that it is a special surprise and that some have stayed behind to show them exactly what is in there and explain what options they have. She then goes to her children, who have been waiting with remarkable patience, and kneels to describe what they found. The children are practically vibrating with excitement. This brings a smile to Elsie's face.

She finds it extremely difficult to understand, though, why this storage room has been here this whole time and no one has touched it. She wants answers. Maybe Farmer Dave will have some idea about it.

She makes her way toward the barn before realizing that once again she is alone. She can't have a repeat of what happened the other day. Luckily, she spots Hope walking in the same direction.

"Hope! Where are you headed?"

"The barn. I'm on animal duty, and I want to get it done as quickly as I can so I can come back and chat with everyone about the room."

"Do you mind if I walk with you? I haven't been to the barn in a couple days. I would like to help out," Elsie says.

"Of course! Let's go." They discuss the room and guess what everyone will vote on, and finally Elsie feels ready to discuss the matter of Mike.

"There's something important I need to talk to you about before we go into the barn," Elsie starts. "The other day, I was in the water filtration room, and I was alone." Hope stops in her tracks and stares at Elsie as if knowing what she is going to say. "Mike attacked me, Hope. He pinned me down and started undressing me. Who knows what would have happened if not for Brian," Elsie says, a tear sliding down her cheek.

"Oh my God, Elsie! I am so sorry. What are you going to do?" Hope asks her quietly.

"That's why I wanted to talk to you. Do you think we should say something? I'm so embarrassed after our talk."

"You should not be embarrassed. If anyone should be, it's me. I should have told someone. Then he wouldn't have done this to anyone else!"

"It isn't your fault either. It's his fault. He's the asshole here. And unfortunately he has a lot of power down here." Elsie considers what to do. "Okay, how about this. We'll wait until this business with the room dies down. Once things are somewhat back to normal, we will have a meeting with the leaders. We'll tell them everything—what happened to you and me. Dr. Simone also knows about what he did to me, so she and Brian will back us up. Then we can all decide what to do with regard to Mike. What do you think?"

"That is a great plan. Or at least the best plan. In the meantime, we go by the buddy system. By the way," Hope adds with a tentative smile as she puts her hand on Elsie's arm, "I love the idea of a party. We haven't had anything to celebrate in so long. It would be nice to pretend like it's old times again, don't you agree?"

"Yes, I think it would be lovely."

When they get to the barn, Elsie excuses herself to speak with Dave.

"Hello, Elsie. How are you?"

"I'm well. I was just curious: How often do you see the Elite?" she asks.

"Once every other week to give them a report on the barn. If we have any issues, I make an appointment to see them sooner, but that hasn't happened in a long time. Why? Did you want an audience with the Elites?"

"No," Elsie says thoughtfully, "but for what reasons could you get me an audience with them?"

"Probably if there was something urgent to discuss. They're actually very busy people. They communicate with the other caverns across the world, you know," Dave says.

Elsie's pulse thunders in her ears. "There are other caverns?" she gasps, even as she realizes that of course there are.

"You think a select few put this place together without telling anyone else? They created underground civilizations internationally. I know they sound pompous to the other folks around here, but they really do care about saving humanity," Dave explains.

"Does everyone know this?" Elsie asks, bewildered.

"I believe so. We don't talk about it, but I'm sure it came up in the beginning."

Elsie decides to just go for it. "Dave, do the Elite live on the bare minimum like we do?"

He frowns. "They don't have balls or banquets with caviar and pheasant, as far as I know. Where are these questions coming from, Elsie?"

"I was just wondering. I'm trying to jog my memory. I'll let you get back to work. Is it okay if I feed the horses?"

"I did put a few apples aside." Dave winks.

"Thank you, Dave. I appreciate it." She grabs the apples by the door and heads over to the stable, pondering what the farmer told her. If Dave is correct about the Elites' intentions, maybe they just lead simple lives dedicated to science and have more supplies than they can ever use. That might explain why the door hasn't opened. She knows none of the people in the cave will risk opening it from on their side. Taking the supplies is bold enough.

Just as Elsie finishes feeding the horses, Hope comes to find her.

"I'm heading back. Did you want to come with me?" she asks.

"Yes, please. I'm dying to know what everyone thinks we should do and what their reactions are!"

When they return to the cavern, most people have taken seats at the tables. The last group is exiting Elsie's would-be cave amid huge smiles and laughter and making their way to join the others. The last to exit are Marjorie, Mira, Carlos, and Angelo. They stride to the front of the room and address the crowd.

"You have all seen now what is behind the wall and what a magical gift we have been given by our benefactors," Carlos begins. Elsie wonders why he's making it sound like the Elite left the room there for them. "It has been proposed that we first have a party and use some of the snacks and food as well as the clothing to celebrate. All in favor of doing this, raise your hands." Hands raise across the room, some people hooting and hollering in agreement.

"Very well," Angelo takes over, calming the crowd. "We will plan the party for two to three nights from now. We'll need five volunteers to put the menu together with Jeremy as well as a list of what we will use from the room with Marjorie. This of course will be after we take inventory. The four of us will take care of that this evening after dinner. If you are interested in volunteering to help with the party planning, please see us after this meeting, and we will put your name in a hat and pull from there."

"After the party, we will have a sign-out sheet for anyone who wants to take something from the 'surplus room,' as we have decided to call it," Mira explains. "I will be in charge of the inventory list. Anything you need from this room, you must see me before taking it. We would like to make everything last as long as possible, and this is the best way to ensure it. Most of the supply will be limited after our party, but we will still have much on reserve. It is important that we behave in a civilized manner and share what we have. There will be no denying anyone anything so long as things are taken in turns. We have decided, if everyone agrees, that the groups you were put in to investigate this room will be the groups by which we divide who is allowed to take from the room on an assigned day."

Marco adds, "Each group will be allowed to take something, one item per person, on their assigned day. So after the party, for example, group three will see Mira, and each person can choose one thing to take for themselves or to share. The following day will be group two, and then the day after that will be group one."

Marjorie then says, "If you object, please raise your hand now, or come see us after this meeting if you would like to remain anonymous."

Most in the room remain quiet and silently nod.

Then a gentleman from the back shouts out, "How are we supposed to trust that no one will go in and just take something out of turn?" Now others are nodding more adamantly.

Angelo steps before the others. "Because we are all going to take turns guarding the entrance in pairs. If we work together and share the responsibility, no one will feel left out or have the need to take more than their fair share."

"I will also be taking inventory at the end of each day to ensure that the numbers match," Mira states confidently. "If they are off, then our system will end, and all the food will be used for communal meals and events. The entrance would then only be guarded by a select few. Let's not work against each other but with each other."

That seems to be enough for the man, who leans back in his chair.

"Wonderful, let's get ready to party!" Marco yells, and the room erupts in shouts and whistles.

CHAPTER NINE

IN THE CENTER of a dark room, on a metal table, a red light blinks on a computer. The door opens, and a man walks in, turning the lights on. The room is white. He is dressed in a white lab coat and medical scrubs. On his lab coat is a symbol: three arrows forming a triangle with a cross in the center.

The room is filled with more computers and screens. On the far wall, four large TV screens flash between different images in black and white. Computers are lined up on the metal table in the center with chairs in front of each. A desk stands at the front of the room, along with a couple of filing cabinets. The man approaches the flashing red light. He then goes to the desk and picks up the phone there.

"This is Terrance in the observatory room. Can you send Lily in as soon as possible? Thank you." He hangs up and returns to the computer, pulling up the image of a room on one of the large TVs. The room has cabinets all around it and large freezers in the center. After a few minutes, people appear on the screen.

A woman enters behind Terrance, dressed in a very impressive white suit. Her auburn hair is done up in a large bun, and she is extremely beautiful.

"You called? What's wrong?"

"The silent alarm was on. It seems we have a breach in supply room eighty-nine." He points to the screen.

"I wonder how in heaven's name they came upon it," she murmurs.

"Should I send anyone there?" Terrance asks.

Lily walks closer to the TV, squinting. "What the hell? How did you get there, Elsie?"

"Ma'am?"

Terrance asks what he should do. Lily stares at the TV for a moment longer and then smiles.

"We have a hundred of these supply rooms, and they have been working so hard." Lily looks to the ground and then back up at Terrance. "Let them alone. Let them enjoy what we have in there. Don't tell anyone of this, and disconnect the feed to this room. I don't want the others knowing about it."

Terrance smiles. "Of course, Ms. Lily. Consider it done." He turns back to his keyboard, and the picture vanishes from the TV, replaced by a feed of the garden room.

CHAPTER TEN

ELSIE SQUEEZES THROUGH the crowd and approaches Angelo.

"I would like to help with the inventory tonight, if that's okay," Elsie says, avoiding his eyes so he doesn't see how distraught she is.

"Don't you want to get some rest? We have to figure out a new spot for your room now," Angelo says.

Elsie feels his eyes on her but simply can't force herself to lift her gaze from the floor. "Well, I want to put my name in to help with the party too, and if I can see what we have and how much, it would be useful for the planning." She decides to go with the truth. "And I really don't want to spend the night alone in the room." If he denies her, she may just ask if she can crash in Andrea's room again.

There's a pause. "Elsie, you've been acting really weird the past couple of days. Are you sure you're okay to do this? Maybe you should rest."

"I'll get some rest before dinner. I will be fine. Please, Angelo, I really want to help." This time she risks meeting his eyes. "Maybe after we inventory the ice cream products we can give some to the kids tomorrow night as a treat. They never get to be kids, and they shouldn't have to wait until the party. It's just a suggestion."

Angelo smiles warmly. "I think it is a very good suggestion, and I'll pass it along to the group after we're done here. I don't think they will object. And I'm fine with you helping out tonight. Go get some rest after you put your name in for the party." She feels him watching her as she turns away.

* * *

Something has gone amiss with Elsie since they broke through the wall. Angelo can't help but grow suspicious again. *Did she somehow guide us to it, a test from the Elites? Will she report what we're taking?* A million uncharitable thoughts fly through his head. He no longer wants to believe that she is working for them, but she's acting so strange. Maybe he will suggest a session with Dr. Simone before she helps with the inventory.

He scans toward the front of the cavern for Dr. Simone and sees that Elsie has already found her. Dr. Simone is rubbing her arm and nodding as they talk at one of the rearmost tables.

Angelo breaks away from the crowd a few minutes later and finds Dr. Simone already close by.

"Oh, hello, Doctor. I saw you talking to Elsie. Where has she gone off to?" he asks.

"She's resting before our session."

"Is everything okay? She seems bothered by something."

"You worry too much. A lot is happening, and it would be overwhelming for anyone. I promise if there is anything else that needs reporting, I will let you know." Dr. Simone pats him on the arm and quickly walks away. Angelo is unconvinced.

* * *

"Just breathe, Elsie, nice and slow," Dr. Simone murmurs.

"I'm trying. When I close my eyes, I see him. I still feel his hands on me and still feel his mouth on mine." Elsie opens her eyes and puts her head between her knees. She abruptly sits up and tries to laugh. "My daydream the other day beats this one a million times over."

"I think you're trying to deal with this trauma the best way you can. Force your mind to think of someone else's face," Dr. Simone suggests.

Elsie closes her eyes again. She sees Mike's face but gives it the boot. She tries to concentrate on the face from her visions: Max's. But somehow it is Angelo who pops into her mind. His deep-brown eyes, calming her. She opens her eyes again and sighs deeply.

"I just can't do it. I can't." She begins to stand, but Dr. Simone stops her.

"Elsie, you can. You are one of the strongest women I have met, and that's saying a lot considering where we are right now. Sit down and try to even your breathing, repeat the colors, and let's see what happens."

Elsie settles obediently and closes her eyes. She pictures the rainbow again. She builds the colors of it behind a bright sun. Her breathing slows.

She is in the water purification room. Max is standing next to her.
"It's beautiful, isn't it?" Elsie gazes at the waterwheel, then at Max.

"It's the most beautiful thing I've seen in the past few weeks." Suddenly they're back at the waterfall by the lake. Rather, they are there for the first time.

"Do you think it's safe to swim in?" Elsie asks hopefully.

"I don't see why it wouldn't be. This place doesn't look to have been affected by anything yet. But let's throw something in and just make sure it doesn't disintegrate." Max grabs a small branch fallen from a large oak tree. He tosses it into the lake. It floats.

"Yay!" Elsie shucks off her clothing. Max laughs as she dives in, popping back up with a happy sigh. "This feels great! I feel like I haven't bathed in years!"

She looks around and doesn't see Max anywhere. She ducks under the water again and when she comes up, she spots Angelo a few feet away, treading water and gazing at her.

Elsie peeks around nervously. "What are you doing here? Where's Max?"

"He's gone, Elsie. Don't you remember? It's just you and me now." He swims over to her and takes her face in his hands. "I promised you I would watch over you now. You don't have to worry about anything anymore." He leans in and kisses her. She kisses him back fiercely, knowing that what he says is true. She feels his hands on her, caressing her. She moves her face away from his and opens her eyes to see Mike holding her.

"What the hell?" she screams.

"I told you it's just you and me, baby."

Immediately Elsie opens her eyes and stands, unsteady on her feet. "I dreamed of that waterfall a couple weeks ago." She drops back down and stares at Dr. Simone, hoping for some sort of explanation.

"Your subconscious is going through a lot right now, Elsie. You can no longer keep your thoughts and emotions separate. I don't think we'll be able to get through to any memories until you sort this out." Dr. Simone rises and moves to sit next to her. "You have to mourn Max properly. You must come to terms with what happened to you with Mike—find closure regarding the decision you made. Finally, you need to resolve these feelings you have for Angelo. I thought it might be because of his indifference to you, but I'm thinking it is much more."

"Please, Dr. Simone; don't tell him any of this. Mourning Max, yes, I can find a way to do that, but the rest . . ." Elsie pauses and remembers Hope. "Dr. Simone, he's done this before. Mike, he, well, he assaulted Hope a couple years ago in the greenhouse. She feels as I do, that nothing can be done given his position in the cavern. We want to wait until things settle. We plan to talk to the leaders after the party and supplies issues are all taken care of. We would need your and Brian's help when speaking with them. We feel strongly about waiting, for now."

"I see," Dr. Simone replies, clearly disturbed. "I have no problem standing by your and Hope's side when that day comes. However, in the meantime, if you face what might have happened if Brian hadn't come in when he did, you may feel differently and speak up sooner. Would you still give him a pass for now? You need to know that either way, what he did was wrong. He assaulted you."

Elsie just drops her head and nods, not agreeing one way or the other. She moves on to Dr. Simone's last recommendation.

"Regarding Angelo, I still don't think he trusts me. I think he's trying. We've had some wonderful conversations and moments, but that's all they are. Just moments. He can't possibly feel the same for me that I think I feel for him." Elsie surprises herself at what she just admitted. She has feelings for him.

"You have some homework, though it would be counterproductive to set a timeline. But once your present issues are addressed, I think only then can you mourn Max the way you need to. Perhaps next week we can try again to access your memories." Dr. Simone looks apologetic, as though she has let Elsie down.

"It's okay, Dr. Simone. I understand. Can we still meet just to talk about everything? Maybe I can face it better."

"Of course, Elsie. I wasn't sure if you were interested in actual therapy with me, but I would be more than happy to work through this with you. I'll see you tomorrow at our usual time." Dr. Simone hugs Elsie, who returns the embrace tightly.

Talk to Angelo first, huh? Elsie thinks as she departs the table. She can do this.

She heads to the other side of the buffet table and sits with Mira, Andrea, and the kids. As they eat their eggs and pancakes for dinner, the air is filled with chitchat.

Angelo is sitting with the leaders as usual, and as usual, Amanda is at a table as well.

"Is everything okay, Elsie? You haven't stopped looking at the front table since we started eating," Mira comments.

"I'm fine. I just think it's weird that Amanda sits at the leaders' table," Elsie says.

"Angelo is there. Wherever he sits, so does she. I keep telling him he needs to make a decision about her." Mira seems to be watching Elsie for a reaction.

"Angelo prefers to worry about his family and everyone else here. He doesn't think he has the time or opportunity to find love. No matter how much Amanda thrusts herself on him," Andrea chimes in with a smile. At that moment, Angelo glances at their table. Elsie quickly looks down at her food and plays with her fork.

After dinner, Elsie joins a small group gathered outside the surplus room, standing alongside Mira.

"Okay, everyone is going to get a clipboard, paper, and pencils. We managed to scrounge some up from our own supply room, amazingly. You will each be assigned an area to inventory. Just write the product name and how many there are. That's it," Angelo says. Marjorie starts handing out the clipboards with the paper and pencils attached to them. Just then, Amanda arrives, hurrying up to Angelo.

"Sorry, I'm here. Will I be working with you, Angelo? You promised," she says.

Angelo looks over to Elsie. "Sure, not a problem. We're going to look through the snack cabinet. This way I can make sure you don't eat any more." He chuckles. She giggles back. So much for Elsie talking to him tonight.

"I'm going to inventory the medical supplies with Dr. Baker. He was a surgeon before all this, and I asked if he could help me identify some of the medication," Mira tells Elsie as Dr. Baker walks up to them.

"Elsie, Angelo asked if you could inventory the freezer with the ice cream. He also said to make sure you choose one type and deduct enough for the children to have tomorrow night. He said it was your idea; I think it's a great one." Marjorie hands Elsie a clipboard with a smile. Gratified, Elsie grins and makes her way inside.

She bends over the ice cream freezer intently, trying to ignore how Amanda keeps putting her hand on Angelo's arm and laughing. He smiles from time to time but is clearly focused on the task at hand. Amanda pulls out items, and he writes them down, ducking back for another look to make sure that Amanda has pulled out all of the items. Elsie smirks to herself, glad she isn't the only one he doesn't trust.

"Everything okay, Elsie?" Marco asks beside her, where he's inventorying the meat freezer.

Elsie pulls her focus back to the freezer. "Yes, I'm just amazed at the variety of ice cream here. I'm not sure which to choose."

"I think kids like the cones. I know I do." He laughs.

"You certainly know the children better than I do, so I will take your advice." Elsie counts the boxes of cones and how many are in each. She then sets aside eight of them for all the children in the cavern—Andrea's three, Dr. Simone and Brian's two, and three others.

"Why aren't there more children?" Elsie asks solemnly. "It's not like they have a life worth living right now, but what happens to the next generation? Does that mean only eight children live in our country right now?"

"I'm not sure, but we can't dwell on things like that. Besides, right now is a happy time. Look at all this great food! I hope they choose steak for our party."

"I hope we all don't get sick from suddenly eating meat," Elsie replies wryly.

Angelo approaches with a smile. "How are things going

over here?"

"We're hoping for steak at the party but also hoping it doesn't give us food poisoning," Marco explains.

"Maybe we can introduce it slowly with other foods. We don't want to stink up the place. How are you both doing with your inventory?" Angelo asks, looking at Elsie. She can't tell if his intensity conveys curiosity or suspicion.

Marco rolls his eyes. "We're doing well, boss. Don't worry, we aren't having too much fun and not getting our work done."

"I was just trying to make small talk. I'll let you guys get back to it then." Angelo returns to Amanda, who is putting back everything they took out to count. They press the vacuum-sealing button and then open up the next cabinet.

"I wish he would just relax already," Marco sighs, shaking his head as he pulls out a package of pork chops. "He's always been serious, but in this world he's all work, no play. I think this party will do him good. He needs to let loose."

"I think a party is just what everyone needs around here," Elsie adds. They continue for the next hour, counting and writing, moving from one area of the freezer to the next. After everyone is done, they give their clipboards to Mira, who looks exhausted and animated at the same time. She and Elsie walk back to the room together for well-deserved rest.

* * *

Elsie is in the cavern, and the tables are set up to display an array of items. There are also racks of clothes filled with beautiful blouses and dresses.

One blouse resembles a traditional Mexican party blouse, white with embroidered flowers. She falls in love with it and calls over to Lydia.

"Okay, what do you want for this blouse? I have to have it!"

Lydia looks at the blouse and then at Elsie. "It is yours for one package of cookies. Preferably chocolate chip, but I'll take whatever you have."

"Deal! I can't wait for Angelo to see this. He'll love it!"

Elsie hands Lydia a package of chocolate chip cookies and removes the blouse from the hanger. She meanders on and sees a table of pictures. One depicts an aerial view of Dallas, and she asks the person behind the table what they want for that picture. The person asks for a bag of chips, and Elsie happily accepts. She looks up and sees Mira at another table, bandaging up one of the children. Her table has medical supplies and medication.

Elsie keeps walking until she comes across a burgundy curtain. She moves it aside and sees Andrea behind the ice cream freezer. She is smiling and telling the children they can only take one each.

"It's a good thing we don't have to trade for ice cream. I would lose all I own with these children," Andrea says. Elsie laughs. She then takes a step back and beholds the marketplace they have created here. She could burst with pride and love. Angelo approaches her.

"Are you ready for our dinner date tonight? I asked Jeremy to make us something special. It cost me a pair of sneakers. It will be worth it, though." Angelo curls his arm around Elsie's waist.

"Yes, I just need to change. I bought the most beautiful blouse from Lydia, and I can't wait to put it on for you! I'll meet you here in ten minutes?"

"I thought we could go for a walk through the garden before dinner, so ten minutes would be great," Angelo replies.

Elsie is woken from her lovely dream by Mira fussing about.

"Sorry, I didn't mean to wake you. I thought I had my other shirt here after the wash, and now I can't find it."

"It's okay. Maybe I'm lying on it?" Elsie rolls over to check and finds Mira's shirt under her blanket bed. "Here. I had the wildest dream."

"Thanks. Really? Do tell!" Mira says excitedly.

Elsie tells Mira her dream, recounting everything *except* the bit about Angelo. Right now she wants to keep that between her and Dr. Simone. But she tells Mira the rest.

"That's a great idea," Mira states. "If you think some sort of market or barter system could work, I would suggest it to Marjorie. Let her go to the other leaders with it. I think she would take to that idea the best."

"I agree. Once we start planning the party, I'll discuss it with her," Elsie decides. She climbs to her feet and gets dressed herself, then washes up and meets Hope at the tunnel entrance for their chores in the water room. At the end of the morning, she's all set to see Dr. Simone. She asks Hope if she would like to join her.

"I told Dr. Simone about what happened to you. Not in detail, but if you want to talk to her . . ."

"I can't. I mean, I've made my peace with it. I just . . . I can't talk about it. It was different with you, but if I have to bring it up again, I would rather just do it the one time with the leaders. If that's okay with you."

"I completely understand. I need to talk to her about a few other things anyway. If you change your mind, though, just come find us at the tables in the main cavern."

"I will." Hope clears her throat. "I hate that he attacked you. I hate that he did that to you. But I am glad I'm not alone anymore with this burden." She stares down at the floor, looking ashamed.

"Don't beat yourself up about it. I feel the same way. I'm glad I am not alone in this and that I have someone to back up my story when I decide to tell it." Elsie hugs Hope. "It's good to have an ally."

* * *

That evening at dinner, Angelo stands and addresses the crowd.

"We are happy to report that we have a healthy amount of snacks and food to be shared for the party and thereafter for about a month, depending on how much we ration ourselves. The volunteers will meet with Marjorie tomorrow around lunchtime to work out the menu and other items. Throughout the day, if you have a moment, stop by the surplus room and see Marjorie for a dress, suit, or something to wear if you would like. We have enough clothing, and the sizes are medium to small. Luckily, we've been largely living off veggies and fruit, so I think we can manage to fit into most of it," Angelo says, chuckling with the others.

He then looks to Elsie. "Finally, if the children will all come up here, we have a surprise. Elsie suggested that the children get a special treat tonight, and we all agreed. So come on up, kids!" he yells. The children scream and cheer and run up to Angelo. As he hands them each an ice cream cone, the older ones begin to cry—happy tears; this is something they vaguely remember and are happy to reunite with. The younger ones seem confused, but once they take a bite, they cry out with delight. It makes Elsie's heart full for the first time in quite a long time.

CHAPTER ELEVEN

ELSIE IS SITTING in a white hospital room. A large man comes in dressed in a gray suit. He approaches her gently.

"*Mon ami,* how are you doing today? I heard you had another round of tests yesterday."

"Yes, Charles, though I don't think they show anything out of the ordinary. Have you heard anything different?" Elsie asks as he takes her hand.

"No, I have not. I wanted to talk to you about these tests. I feel that we may have to take more drastic measures, perhaps some biopsies. I have spoken—"

He is interrupted by the woman named Lily, who is dressed in a white suit.

"Charles. What, may I ask, are you doing here today?" she asks, her tone icy.

"I was just here going over our options with Elsie. You can't fault me for filling her in on what we think is best," Charles explains.

"What *you* think is best, Charles." She commands the room with her presence. Charles is a large man, but he seems so small with her here.

"I want to do whatever is best for our people, for humanity. No matter what it is," Elsie interjects.

"Not at the ultimate cost to you, Elsie. I will not allow it, nor will the council."

* * *

Elsie jolts up from her spot on the floor. This dream is new. She has never seen the man before. *Is it from my memory?* There is only one way to find out. She rises and sees that Angelo and Marco have left and Mira is washing up.

"Good morning. How did you sleep?" Mira asks.

"Very well, thanks. Have you seen Dr. Simone? I need to talk to her."

"You look like you've seen a ghost. Is it Max? Did you have a dream about him?" Mira looks concerned.

"No, something else. I'll fill you in once I speak to her. I just want to make sure it wasn't a dream."

Elsie finds the doctor leaving her room with Brian and gives her a hasty greeting. The doctor kisses her husband's cheek before he heads off to the entrance with their children.

"I was hoping we could have a quick session. I think I had a memory last night," Elsie says in a rush.

"Absolutely. Shall we sit at the tables?"

Elsie walks to the main area with Dr. Simone, recounting everything from her dream.

"It doesn't seem real at all. Like the memory of Max. But somehow, I know they are mine. I was thinking, while it is still fresh, I could try to remember it again to see if it was just a dream or something in my subconscious."

"Well, let's give it a go. I will certainly not refuse you if you feel you are ready."

They sit across from each other, and Elsie closes her eyes. She begins her breathing and her counting. She builds her rainbow. One time, then two times.

She is in a room with an MRI machine, being pulled out of it. A handsome blond doctor with bright-green eyes enters with the large gentleman, Charles.

"See anything worth mentioning? Like little aliens controlling my breathing?" Elsie says, joking and somewhat hopeful.

"Nothing out of the ordinary. Well, pre-ordinary, I guess. Most people have some lung damage. Your lungs are completely clear. No damage whatsoever," the handsome young doctor explains.

"Which means there is something more we need to find, Elsie," Charles says.

Elsie sighs. "I'll do anything I can, but between the blood tests, MRIs, and CAT scans, I don't know what more there is."

"One step at a time, Elsie. We can't rush this. It's too important. Why don't you get dressed while Charles and I talk about our next steps?"

While Elsie dresses, she overhears some of their conversation.

"A biopsy is the only thing left," Charles says sternly.

"A biopsy is invasive and dangerous. We don't know that she could survive it, and I don't think it is fair to ask her to try."

"This is for our survival! I will not stop for anything or anyone until we find a reason or cure. We cannot stay locked up here forever!" Charles shouts, and a door slams. Elsie emerges in her ASU T-shirt and jeans.

"The only thing left to do is too dangerous to do?" Elsie asks the doctor.

"I won't allow it, Elsie. I will go to the council and discuss it with them. There must be another way that isn't dangerous to you," he says firmly.

"I will do whatever it takes to save the world. I don't have anything else to live for. It's fine.' Elsie looks to the ground.

"You have me, Elsie. And you have a life to live for, and I won't take that from you."

Her vision becomes hazy. Elsie is brought back to Dr. Simone.

"How did that feel?" Dr. Simone asks, hopeful.

"I wish I knew what this all meant. It was a memory; I vaguely remember it. It feels less like a movie but not as clear as the one I had the other day. I don't even know for sure what I was being tested on or what for. I assume it has to do with my breathing the air, but we don't know for certain. This is so crazy." Her eyes grow teary. Dr. Simone regards Elsie earnestly and takes her hand.

"I think you must talk to Angelo. Just you. Tell him what you have seen and tell him how you feel. You need help, but maybe it is help I can't give you right now. Maybe he can."

"I know."

When Elsies reaches the entrance to the surplus room, she finds Angelo sitting in the opening, taking the first guard shift.

"Hi, I heard you were here," she begins, gathering her courage.

He stands and narrows his eyes. "I was hoping you would stop by," he says much more forcefully than she expected. "I need to know, Elsie, how did you know about this extra supply room?"

She protests, "I didn't." At his glare she babbles, "It was a coincidence. I swear to you, I had no idea this was here." Elsie steps up to him, imploring him to believe her.

"You chose this cave. You suggested we dig back and forth. Why not go straight back? And then after we found the room, you started to act weird. Don't you understand how that would look to me?" he demands, his voice rising.

Tears abruptly fill her eyes. She wants so badly for Angelo to trust her, and on the cusp of finally convincing herself to open up, their relationship is going backward. She fights back the tears but can't say anything in her defense past the knot in her throat.

"I don't know what it is you're up to. I don't understand what you want from us. If this is all a game to you, please just go back to where you came from and leave us be," Angelo yells.

"*I have nowhere to go!*" Elsie shouts at him. "Why can't you see I just want to help? I want to survive just like you!" Now she's openly crying as Angelo shouts back.

"You are not one of us, Elsie. No one knows who you are and what you want, apparently not even you, which I don't believe for one minute."

Elsie sees red with frustration and screams, "How many times do we have to discuss this? I can't remember, and it scares me that I can't. Every memory I have feels like I am watching a foreign film! All I want to do is help and be useful!"

"You have given me *no reason* to trust you!"

Elsie catches her breath and grits out, "I have given you no reason not to."

A breathless pause follows. Then, suddenly, Angelo presses his mouth to hers. Her arms involuntarily go to his neck and her hands to his hair. *What is happening?* she wonders mindlessly. She doesn't want it to end. But it does end, as quickly as it began. Angelo stares into her eyes, mumbles an apology, and leaves.

Elsie is frozen in place for what feels like hours. One minute Angelo is shouting at her, making her feel completely unwelcome, and in the next he is holding her as if he never wants her to go. She sits at the entrance to the surplus room, going over it again and again until Marco comes and relieves her. Then she runs to the friend she hopes will help her make sense of all this.

* * *

"Seriously, Angelo, what are you doing here? I know this is the very last place on earth you want to be," Mira says as Angelo shucks peas at her side.

"What, now I can't help you? I got done with my chores early, so

I thought I would come here." Angelo tries to sound logical but does not make eye contact with Mira.

She eyes him doubtfully. "What did you do? I can tell something is up."

"I don't know what you're talking about." Angelo slowly and methodically works through the pea pods.

"You're here because you want to talk to me about something and you don't know how to begin." She continues to stare at him. "Is it about Elsie? Do you feel embarrassed because you're starting to realize that you like her!" Mira whispers gleefully.

Angelo sighs. "I got into a fight with her. I think she knew about the surplus room and led us to it. I don't know yet why, but I confronted her about it."

"Oh, Angelo." Mira drops her elbows to the table to put her head in her hands.

"But then she came up to me, and, well . . ." Angelo clears his throat. "I kissed her." He stares down at the table again like a schoolboy caught smoking in the bathroom.

"Oh. My. God!" Mira screeches. "I knew it! I knew it!!"

"Keep it down, Mira. I don't know what it means." Angelo slams a pod down on the table. "I still don't know if I trust her. But she makes me feel . . . I don't know." He resumes shucking the peas. "She probably hates me right now. I kissed her, and I was so confused, I just apologized and walked away."

Mira takes Angelo's hand into hers. "Angelo, it has been a very long time since anyone has met someone new and found love. Maybe what you are feeling is guilt. Don't sabotage yourself for the rest of us. We will thrive one day. I am confident the air will clear, and we'll all leave and find more people. I know our day will come. Your day has already come, Angelo, with her, and we are very happy for you." She releases his hand and continues with her work. "Now, you be happy for you. Go to her. Let her know that now you *do* trust her, with your life."

Angelo stares at Mira in disbelief. "I know nothing about her. She knows nothing about herself, yet she manages to find a supply room? I don't think it *is* guilt, Mira. I think it's common sense. I just don't know how to move past it and let my heart take over."

Mira glares at her brother. "You do know her. The two of you have been getting to know each other for days now. You know she is an angel sent to help us through our darkest days. She is the light at the end of the tunnel, and the sooner you see that, the easier it will be for you to be with her. Stop questioning everything. Just go with it. Follow your heart. You know that's what you want to hear, or you wouldn't have come to me with this. I know you hate peas. So go now. But clean your room, first; you're going to need it for later." She winks at him.

"*Ay*, Mira." He shakes his head but gets up to leave. He doesn't know when or why it happened, but Mira is right, and he can't deny his heart any longer. He is falling in love with Elsie. Love that he has confused for mistrust and disdain—a realization he needs to convey to her. Hopefully, she doesn't slap him in the face.

* * *

Elsie sits quietly in Andrea's room as the children play out front. She has no idea how to broach the subject.

Andrea returns with hot water and lemon. Elsie is sure that even with the various teas in the surplus room, Andrea will continue to use her own simple recipe.

"Well, something important is on your mind. I don't think you've ever sat this long this quietly. Usually you have twenty questions that need answers," Andrea says matter-of-factly.

"How do you know when someone likes you? Even if they don't say nice things to you?" Elsie asks plaintively.

"Usually that *is* how you know," Andrea chuckles. "Boys are mean to hide their true feelings. Why? Is Angelo being particularly mean to you?"

Elsie straightens in her seat. "How do you know I'm speaking about Angelo? I'm sure there are a few people here who don't like me."

"Everyone here likes you. Some may not trust you completely, but none of them voice it as forcefully as Angelo does. Has he confronted you again?" Andrea asks.

"He did. Then he kissed me!" Elsie's cheeks grow hot. "And I felt what I can only imagine is equivalent to an electric shock through my whole body." She takes a deep breath.

Andrea nods and smiles. "Yes, he likes you, Elsie. We all saw this coming. Do you like him?"

Elsie sits for a moment, pondering this question. She knows she does; her dreams and visions have confirmed this. "When he's near me, I feel drawn to him. I want to be next to him. However, when he pushes me away, emotionally, it hurts." She puts her palm to her chest. "But when he kissed me, I wanted his body to melt into mine and never let go. That could mean I like him," Elsie says sarcastically. Then tears form again in her eyes. "Ugh!"

"No, dear. It does not mean you like him." Andrea tilts her head toward her new friend. "It means you are falling in love with him."

"Do you love Marco? Does Marco love you?" Elsie asks curiously, seizing on the distraction.

"It's hard for me. I had a great love with my husband, Sergio. My world moved for him and his for me. That is love, Elsie. Love is when you would shift your entire existence, when you would give your life for someone else. When he died, I thought my world was over. But I had to live for my babies, and that is what I did. I survived for my children."

She gazes down into her teacup. "Marco makes me feel things I have not felt for a very long time. But I don't want to forget the love I had for my husband. And Marco is younger than I and has more options in front of him Or his lack of options now might be part of what pushes him to me. He is very good to me, but I do not want to mistake that for more than what it is: a deep and lasting friendship."

When Andrea finally looks up, a tear drips from her eyelashes. "Our circumstances are different. Trust me when I say you don't want to sit around and ponder what Angelo's feelings might be. Go and ask him. Talk to him and let him know how you feel. I am certain you will be happy with his answer for you. If you aren't, you come right here to me, and we will cry over an ice cream bar together!" She smiles.

When Elsie gets to their room, she finds Mira waiting, along with an outfit on the mattress: a black tank top embroidered with colorful flowers and denim shorts.

"I borrowed these from Lydia. When you told me your dream, I remembered she had something similar to what you described. She's had them since she got here. I thought you could wear this when you talk to Angelo," Mira chirps.

"I don't know what you think you know," Elsie begins.

"I know enough to know that the two of you should stop these games. Stop trying to push each other away and embrace each other, literally!" Mira stamps her foot.

"I don't want to push him away. I just . . . I-I don't know what to do or say. I feel like he hates me one minute, but then not quite the next. I'm incredibly confused," Elsie admits.

"He doesn't hate you. If you wear this, bat your eyelashes, and tell him the truth, you will see exactly how much he does *not* hate you! I promise." The other girl ends with one of her charming smiles and sashays out of the room.

Elsie doesn't change her pants. She does change her shirt, though. The tank top plunges a little low in the front, but it isn't too revealing. Maybe it could work in her favor. She hears someone in Angelo's room and takes a peek. Angelo is pacing back and forth, mumbling to himself. Elsie clears her throat to ask permission to enter. Angelo waves her in.

"I'm glad you're here. I wanted to talk to you about before. I'm truly sorry."

She looks away, her eyes prickling at the memory. "I wish I could prove to you that I am who I am. I swear I'm not working for the Elites, that I knew nothing about the surplus room. I am just a girl who is lost."

Angelo steps in front of her. "Elsie, it was wrong of me to accuse you. I really am sorry for what I said. When it comes to you, I'm on a seesaw. One minute I am so confused by you, scared of you. The next I just want to be near you." He looks at the floor. The tops of their heads touch.

"That kiss . . . I liked it. A lot. I want to do it again." She looks up at him longingly. When Angelo raises his face to meet her eyes, she hesitantly lifts her arms to his shoulders and brings her lips to his. This kiss is softer, slower. There is no anger or urgency to it. It is full of feeling and wanting.

Angelo grips her waist and moves his hands under her top, caressing her back. Elsie moans, breathing in the scent of him—of soil and stone. She feels like her body is on fire and Angelo is the only one who can put it out.

As their kiss deepens, so does her desire. She is certain that even as far back as she *can't* remember, she has never felt this way. Angelo pulls her tank top over her head and kisses her neck, laying her back on his recliner—and they pause and laugh at the awkward position.

"I guess I didn't think this through." He gazes at her with heat and passion and kisses her again, working the recliner lever with a sudden lurch and another laugh. Then he undoes the button of her jeans, and she wiggles out of them. She has no clue if she knows what she's doing, but it doesn't matter. As Angelo kisses down her body, Elsie gasps in exhilaration. But when he stands back and pulls off his own clothes, her vision briefly clouds over with fear, the memory of the last time she was in this position flashing through her mind. She looks off to the corner.

Angelo frowns with concern. "Do you want me to stop? I'm sorry; I should have thought—"

"Don't stop, Angelo. I want this. I want you."

He gently lowers on top of her, and she moves eagerly against him.

She hopes no one can hear; she doesn't want to share this moment or him with anyone else. It seems so natural and yet so foreign at the same time. Her body knows what to do even if her mind is a minute slower, and she is certain there should be fireworks exploding above them.

Later, Angelo lies next to her, his leg wrapped around her as if to protect her from the world. He kisses her forehead, then her nose, then kisses her lips as softly and passionately as he did when they first began.

She smiles. "I never knew I could feel like this. Not only in my heart but in my whole body!"

"I never want to know this feeling with anyone but you, Elsie. I am so sorry for how I started things off between us. You scare me. Not just because we don't know much about you; it scares me how you make me feel this way."

"I never want anything but good for your people. For our people. I promise you that I will never do anything intentionally to hurt you or your family." She snuggles closer. "I just wish we could stay like this forever."

"For now we can. Right now, let's just lie here in each other's arms and dream about a life together. We may have to bargain with Mira or Marco for a mattress, though," he says, laughing quietly. "I don't think we can share this recliner every night without killing our backs."

Elsie rests her head on his chest.

"I will share any space with you so long as I can be in these arms."

With that they both fall into a slumber, the best Elsie has had in months.

* * *

The next morning, Angelo awakens and slides out from under Elsie. He slips on his jeans quietly so as not to wake her, then shuffles into their common area for a glass of water. Marco is sitting at the table.

"Since when do you sleep without your nightshirt?" Marco looks his brother over. "There's something different about you."

Elsie emerges wearing her jeans and the first thing she could grab, Angelo's shirt. It hangs from the arms and down to her knees. Marco takes a look at her and says, "Ohhh," and smiles. He grabs a granola bar. "Okay, you two, don't wait too long to get to your stations. People will start to talk." And he walks out laughing hysterically.

Angelo shakes his head. "I'm sorry he was here. I probably should have left your shirt a little closer to you."

"It's not even my shirt. Mira gave it to me to talk to you with." Elsie shrugs. "I guess it was a good idea."

Angelo takes a moment to appreciate her beauty with a happy sigh and pulls her to him, kissing her. "Good morning."

"Good morning." She smiles into the kiss. "Marco is correct, though. We should get ready. Hope will be waiting for me. I also want to meet with Marjorie today. I have some ideas I want to go over."

"Oh?" Angelo asks with some wariness. He has to admit the changes she's introduced thus far have been good, but change can be exhausting.

"Don't worry; I'll talk to you about it afterward. Just some ideas on how to bring back some civilization. There's something else I wanted to discuss concerning my session with Dr. Simone. Maybe we can talk about it over dinner tonight? Just me and you?"

"That is an amazing idea." And he leans in to kiss her again.

"*Yes!*" They turn to see Mira dancing in the opening to their cave suite. "Marco said there was a sight to see, and I hoped it was this!" She hops over and bumps Elsie's hip with her own. "I just wanted to grab a bar and head out. I suggest the two of you do the same. After you dress, of course."

Elsie rolls her eyes. "Thank you, Mira."

"I'll see you both later then. Oh, and, Mira, we may have to discuss the sleeping arrangements later today," Angelo says as he grabs a bar and heads back into his room.

* * *

"I have to get to the prepping room, but I want *all* the details later!" Mira jumps up and down. "Well, maybe not all the details." She shudders as she grabs her bar, then hip-bumps Elsie again.

Elsie's thoughts have already shifted focus as she ponders the ideas she wants to share with Marjorie.

As she heads out to the main cavern after getting dressed, Elsie sees Angelo has been sidetracked by Amanda. She is rubbing her hand over his arm and smiling flirtatiously. She licks her lips and laughs, and Angelo laughs with her. He almost seems more affectionate, not less.

Elsie realizes she has stopped in her tracks. The roller coaster of emotions she has ridden over the past weeks takes a steep plunge. A thousand thoughts chase each other through her mind, but what rises to the top is *What was I thinking? That he would change his mind about me in a few hours?* A wash of red floods Elsie's mind, her ears, her eyes. She doesn't hear Mira calling her or see Angelo looking confused.

Elsie runs. She runs through the opening that led her here. She runs back to where she thinks she came from. She just wants out. And she wants Angelo to get what he wants. If he wants her gone, then she will go.

Elsie confronts the metal doorway. Time to test her memories. Time to see if she can breathe.

Elsie pushes the door with all her might and flings herself into a shallow airlock while others call her name. She slams the first door shut and pushes at an identical one, securely shutting it behind her before running into a deserted road. The air is thick and yellowish orange. Elsie thinks back to Angelo laughing with Amanda and doesn't pause to gradually test her theory. With tears in her eyes, she runs.

* * *

Angelo looks up when Mira cries Elsie's name and sees Elsie pelting toward the exit. Mira gives him a stern look and gestures toward Amanda. His realization is instantaneous. *Does Elsie really think me so heartless?* Why would he leave her to go directly into the arms of another woman?

But it doesn't matter how Elsie could believe that of him. If he doesn't get to her now, he might lose her forever.

Instinctively, he chases her into the tunnel, followed by Mira, Amanda, and a few others. Then he hears the slamming of metal, and his heart drops into his stomach.

She wouldn't.

She would.

Angelo charges up the incline toward the metal door.

Mira tries to grab his hand. "*No*, Angelo, no!"

"She'll die out there!" Angelo hollers, straining to open the first door.

"That was her choice! You don't have to die for her!" Amanda shouts.

Angelo looks back at Amanda and then Mira. "Yes, I do." He shoves the door open and jumps through as Mira yells after him.

Quickly moving through the airlock and outside, he covers his face with his shirt and begins jogging, hoping this direction is the right one. His lungs tighten. If he doesn't find her soon, they will both be lost to the atmosphere.

He thinks he sees her in the distance and tries to call out her name, choking as he does. She's heading into the abandoned town where the cavern citizens first gathered tools, clothing, and other supplies. It has been quite some time since they last ventured out there.

Ten minutes pass. Twenty. His movements are sluggish now. His lungs feel like rocks, but he finds the strength to continue. He has to get to her. Though his throat is burning, he calls for her again and again, veering toward the hospital. He can barely lift his feet. He wheezes one final time, "Elsie, please." And then his vision grows fuzzy, and everything goes dark.

* * *

Elsie crumples in front of an abandoned hardware store and begins to cry in great, heaving sobs. Just as she prepares to dive into her darkest, most self-derisive thoughts and be swallowed by them, she is struck by a realization.

She can breathe. She's not even struggling. She feels perfectly fine.

Does this mean the air has become breathable again? Or was her memory correct? Can she breathe air that should be killing her? She stands with a glimmer of hope in her heart, a glimmer that distracts from the angst and grief. She can't wait to let everyone know! Her personal problems don't matter a whit right now.

She starts back down the street back to the cavern and hears her name, then terrible coughing. *Angelo.* He came out for her but didn't make it as far. She runs faster, thankful for the breath giving her the momentum she needs. She comes to an abrupt stop when she finds him lying on the ground. Dropping to her knees, she lifts his head and listens. He's still breathing, but his breath is dreadfully shallow. She looks around, frantic.

"Breathe, Angelo, breathe!" she cries. *Why would he come out after me? Why would he risk his life for me?* Andrea's words come back full force: *"That is love, Elsie. Love is when you would shift your entire existence, when you would give your life for someone else."* Now Angelo is giving his life, and she must save it.

Across the intersection is an abandoned hospital. *There must be something in there I can use to save him.* She stands and pulls at his arm to drag him toward the building, but she doesn't have the strength. Hoping the hospital might have a backboard or other material to drag him on, she runs toward the front door, which displays a familiar symbol: three arrows in a triangle with a cross in the middle.

The front doors open automatically, accompanied by a beeping noise, almost like a timer, and she darts through just as the doors close.

The hospital is far from abandoned.

In the lobby, a couple of men in white lab coats stare at her, whispering. They look confused. A woman sitting behind the front desk grabs a walkie-talkie, and Elsie hears quick footsteps echoing from far away.

"Please, I need help. That man out there, he collapsed. He can't breathe," Elsie cries. Another man in a white coat appears from the hallway. He has wavy blond hair and green eyes.

He approaches her calmly and says, "Elsie? What are you

doing here?"

The past five years flood back with the force of a slap. Her head throbs under the onslaught.

At the center of her most recent memories is this man.

"Cameron?" she asks before her vision is enveloped in darkness.

CHAPTER TWELVE

MARCO BURSTS INTO Andrea's room. "My brother is gone! He ran outside after Elsie!" The children are playing cards on the floor and look up at him in alarm. Andrea rises from her chair, bewildered.

"What are you talking about?"

"My brother and Elsie were together last night, and something spooked Elsie this morning, and she ran out of the tunnels! She ran outside, and Angelo ran after her! Mira is a mess, and I don't know what to do!"

Andrea takes Marco's hand. "It will be okay," she says with absolute certainty. Rumor has it that Elsie can breathe outside, and Andrea knows Elsie will not let anything happen to Angelo. "Where is Mira now?"

"Marjorie is looking after her. What was he thinking? Why the hell would he go after her?" Marco shakes his head at Andrea.

"He loves her, Marco." *Enough is enough.* "If I ran out . . . if I ran out, would you come for me?"

Marco takes her other hand. "I wouldn't hesitate. I would run to the end of the earth to bring you back."

"I have faith that they will find each other and make it back. Maybe a little worse for wear, but in my heart, I know they will be fine."

He seems to take heart from her steady gaze.

"Oh, for heaven's sake, Mommy, please just kiss him!" Tabby shouts. They stare at her as Elton and Zander giggle. Marco looks back at Andrea, and she smiles.

With that, he takes her in his arms and kisses her. She lets him. It is a sweet kiss filled with all the love and devotion he has for her. The children cheer.

"I should get back to Mira and Marjorie. I'll keep you posted and see you later this evening." He turns to the opening but then stops and kisses her again. "I love you, Andrea," he says.

Fighting back her fears, Andrea nods. "I know, Marco. I love you too."

Marco finds Mira bawling her eyes out and Marjorie trying to comfort her.

"What could he have been thinking? I know he loves her, but to leave us all like that? They are both going to die out there!" Mira cries again.

"Mira, we must hope that he will find her in time and bring her back. Maybe the air has improved and they will have a little more time."

"Marjorie, it's been over an hour! They . . ." Mira doesn't finish.

Marco stands back, knowing that what Mira can't say is most likely the truth: If they aren't back by now, they are not coming back. Yet he feels now as Andrea does—that they made it through. That somehow, they both are hiding out somewhere, safe and sound.

* * *

"Please, just explain this all to me. I'm having trouble grasping it. I thought everyone was underground. How long have you been here?" Angelo asks between lungfuls of oxygen. He came to moments ago to find this Adonis of a doctor holding Elsie's hand at the hospital bed next to his. "How do you know Elsie? Why are we not choking to death now like I almost did outside?"

Energized by the mystery of this place, Angelo chances rolling out of bed. He stands and moves to Elsie's bedside, taking her other hand to show that his feelings for Elsie may just be stronger than this doctor's. The doctor, who introduces himself as Cameron, eyes him mistrustfully, then clears his throat as if gearing up for a long explanation.

"After the Elite created the tunnels and caverns, they wanted a base of operations. We eventually developed a way to recirculate the air not only in the caverns but in a building. We had enough equipment for one building, so the hospital was the logical choice. It has rooms for us to live, a kitchen, laboratories, and supplies. We retrieve supplies from the tunnels as we run low.

"We have been trying to restore the air quality with artificial rains, large agricultural fans, so on and so on. Nothing has worked. One day, a man named Charles came to us with this girl that was found during a scavenger run to the hardware store. She was in bad shape, but it wasn't from the air quality. She was thin, malnourished, exhausted. We took her in and got her healthy."

Cameron regards Elsie longingly.

"Once she was healthy. We asked her how she came here, and she said she walked. Can you believe that? She said she walked, like it was no big deal that she could breathe the air that would kill the rest of us." He shakes his head and chuckles. "That's Elsie, though."

Angelo is far from amused by this doctor's puppy-dog eyes.

"So, in between having her do busywork in the labs to keep her close but productive, we would test her. Blood tests, MRIs, endoscopies, you name it. But nothing came back conclusive. I was about to give up when Charles demanded more tests. He wanted to induce a coma and then dissect her. Biopsy her lungs and other organs to find out once and for all why she can breathe while the rest of us choke and die.

"I have done a lot in the name of science. Some things might even be considered questionable. But I was not going to kill this woman." Cameron strokes Elsie's hand.

"So you used her like a guinea pig, poking and prodding her to find a cure. You made her a lab rat," Angelo accuses.

"No, she volunteered. Well, I let her believe she had a choice, and she wanted to help people. She said, 'If I can save humanity, then so be it!' She thought she could be the answer. I honestly think she would have given her life as well if I had told her what Charles wanted from her."

Angelo shakes his head, finally lowering his hackles enough to appreciate the doctor's concern for Elsie. "Sounds like Elsie. What did you do, exactly?"

"We have at our disposal a serum that numbs the memory center of the brain. It was originally developed for Alzheimer's studies, to try to revive the memory, but it had the opposite effect. So the serum was used to help patients with PTSD. It worked wonders. Patients with PTSD were forgetting their trauma and living normal lives. Of course, the serum was still in testing when all this"—he gestures out the window at the yellowed landscape—"happened. So we shelved it for future use.

"When I was approached to give Elsie the medication to induce the coma, I gave her the memory serum instead. I gave her what I judged to be enough to block out the past five years. The night after I gave it to her, I took her to your cavern and placed her inside. I knew your people would care for her."

Elsie stirs. "Oh, my head," she says, slowly rising to a sitting position.

"Elsie, my God. I was so worried." Angelo kisses her forehead. Elsie opens her eyes and smiles, and Cameron releases her hand.

Elsie turns to the doctor. "Cameron. Hi." Her smile fades. "Did

I overhear that you gave me a memory serum? Why wouldn't you tell me?"

He regards her with mournful adoration. "I wanted to keep you safe. I knew you wouldn't leave on your own—that you would allow yourself to be tested. So I did what I thought best. I didn't tell anyone what I did. I'm glad you're back, and I'm sorry." Cameron drops his gaze.

"I understand why you did it. I was so gung-ho to prove Max saved me for a purpose that I didn't think my life was worth living if I couldn't help. But that was before." Angelo is relieved by the loving look she gives him then. "Things are different now."

"Do you remember anything?" Cameron asks.

"When I saw you, it all came back." To Angelo she says, "It isn't a movie anymore. I remember." Her eyes seem to lose focus.

Cameron nods. "As I said before, this serum was in testing. It was discovered that in a few patients, a trigger could bring their memories back. Researchers were working on how to bypass the triggers, but again, it was shelved before we could do more testing."

Elsie refocuses on Angelo. "I was in my senior year at Arizona State when the bombs went off in all the major cities. When I heard Dallas was hit, I had to get there. That's where my family was. They said there were very few survivors, but I was determined to find them. I hitchhiked, rode on buses, trucks, whatever I could do to get there. When I did get there, everything was decimated. But I refused to give up hope. I went to my grandmother's apartment building and found it was standing, barely. I ran up to her apartment and found her dead inside. I took her hand and cried. I didn't want to leave, but the building was shaking, and someone grabbed me and dragged me out of there."

"Max?" Angelo asks. She nods.

"We got about two blocks away when the building came down. He told me we should stay together, and we looked for other survivors. We did find some, others searching for loved ones. But they started to get sick, coughing and choking. They would fall right where they stood. Max started getting sick, so he and I decided to go west, thinking we could escape the bad air. As we traveled, we found more of the same, more people coughing and dying. All the buses and trains had stopped running, but we kept walking.

"Bombs were hitting other cities. We knew it was a matter of time before we suffocated too. Max couldn't move fast, so it was hard to get ahead of the worst of it. It took us days to go miles. We ate what we could find. We slept only when we couldn't move anymore. We finally came upon this town, and Max succumbed. And, well, you know what happened then. I was so tired and hungry; we hadn't found food in weeks."

Elsie breaks off, tears running down her cheeks. Angelo grasps her hand. She wipes her face with her other hand and continues, "That's when someone found me and brought me here. I'm sure Cameron filled you in on the rest." She stares at Cameron. "I can't be the only one, can I? The only person on the planet that can breathe?"

"There she is! Where have you been, *mon ami*? We were so worried when you left us!" A burly man storms in, shouting in a French accent. He has white pants and a white jacket with a light-blue shirt, and his hair is thinning around a plump, round face.

"Charles, she's in delicate condition. I think it best you wait until tomorrow," Cameron begins, but the other man is clearly too excited to see Elsie and pushes him aside.

"Where did you go? I was so worried." Charles sits close to Elsie.

"I don't remember. I wandered into a cavern and must have hit my head; I lost my memory. This is Angelo. He cared for me. Angelo, this is the man who brought me to Cameron after I was found." Something in her eyes puts Angelo on high alert.

"Yes," Angelo confirms. "She seems to have wandered off again, and I came to bring her back home with me." He wants to make it clear that she is not staying.

Charles seems to smirk at him. "How very brave of you, going out into the open air to find our little flower."

"Charles, I have some ideas after spending time with the people in the caverns. I believe there are changes that might benefit everyone. Please, can I speak with the council?" Elsie asks. Angelo is confused. They should not be staying here. They need to get back to their cavern.

"All in good time, *mon ami*. You need to rest now. It seems you have had quite an adventure. Cameron, make sure that she gets a good rest tonight. Give her something so that she sleeps well," the big man says meaningfully. Angelo is about to protest when they are interrupted by a woman's voice.

"Don't be silly, Charles. Elsie seems fine, and I believe the council would love to hear what she has to say." A woman, also clad in white, enters the room. She has a strong Australian accent and seems familiar. *She must be one of the celebrities*, Angelo thinks. Cameron looks relieved. "Just because you were the one to pull her into the fold over a year ago does not mean that you have the right to decide what is best for her."

"You are forgetting how important it is for her to rest, so that we can get the information she can provide," Charles simpers.

Lily gives him a very stern look. "And you forget that there are other ways to get the information you so desire."

"I'm not stupid, Charles," Elsie interjects. "I know you want to cut me up." Charles all but rears back, his face turning red. "But I want to talk to the council first. After that, I will make the decision whether to be put on a table and cut up into pieces!"

Angelo is aghast at her matter-of-fact manner. "Over my dead body."

"Elsie, you can't be serious," Cameron protests at the same time.

Lily gestures at them to be quiet. "Men, this lies under my decision-making capacity. No one is putting her on a table and cutting her up!" She turns to Elsie with a nurturing tone. "Elsie, we don't know why you have this gift, but it may just be an anomaly.

It is possible that nothing you do or allow us to do to you will save anyone. I will escort you to the council myself so that you can speak with them."

"I'm going too," Cameron and Angelo say in unison. They eye each other uneasily.

Charles huffs, "I will alert the council to an important meeting in the morning. I hope you know what you're doing, Lily. There is much we could learn from this flower."

"And there is much we could suffer in destroying it." Lily turns to Elsie again. "I will make sure you are safe until the meeting. Cameron, please get Elsie and our guest something to eat. I'm going to check on something right outside the door here. Give you two time to talk." She smiles as she exits the room.

Angelo is surprised when the first thing Elsie has to say when they are alone is an angry "What were you thinking coming out after me?!"

He merely smiles at her. "You didn't know you could breathe the air. What were you thinking?"

Elsie looks embarrassed. "I saw you with Amanda, and I just . . . I don't know, I felt like you played me, so that you could hurt me and get rid of me, and I don't *know* why I thought that! It was irrational, and"—she looks into his eyes—"it was foolish. I ran because I was hurt. And because I would rather die than live without you, so it seemed like the time to test whether I could breathe out here."

Angelo takes her gently into his arms. "And I ran after you because I would rather die than live without you. I was laughing with Amanda because for the first time in a long time, I am happy. *You* make me happy. So I guess we are both extremely foolish people." He smiles as he kisses her. He then pulls back. "What is the story with you and Cameron, though. He seems very attached to you."

Elsie blushes. "I know Cameron liked me, and I felt very close to him. If I hadn't left, I don't know what would have happened between us, but I never felt about him the way I feel about you, Angelo."

Angelo's heart flutters. "I am glad you left this place. And I never felt about Amanda an iota of what I feel for you." He kisses her deeply and pulls her tight against him. They are interrupted by Cameron clearing his throat and entering with a tray.

"Sorry to interrupt, but I got your food."

"Thank you, Cameron."

He sets the tray on the side table. It holds sandwiches and salads.

"Are these from the tunnels? How do you get your food? I never thought to ask," Elsie asks.

"We have a rotating schedule for those who venture to the tunnels to collect food. That reminds me, Angelo, although you came to us in bad shape, you were still breathing. I wonder if you may have some of the qualities that Elsie has, to have survived so long on the surface."

Angelo shakes his head. "I was struggling to breathe. It was my determination to find her that kept me going. You are *not* using me as a pin cushion to find out what 'abilities' I have. I would have died if Elsie hadn't found me."

Cameron continues, "But it didn't take much oxygen to revive you. I only ask that you let me take a blood sample. No one has asked me to do it. I would merely like to compare it to Elsie's to see if anything stands out. This is for all humankind."

Elsie turns to Angelo, her eyes hopeful. "No one can make you do anything. But if we can help find a way to let everyone breathe, wouldn't you want that for our people? For your sister, brother, and everyone else?"

She cuts right to the core. He sighs. "One blood test; that's all. And it has to be now. I'm not waiting around after she meets with the council to continue being your test subject."

"It's a deal." Cameron immediately crosses the room to rummage inside a cabinet, returning with a blood collection kit. Angelo doesn't take his eyes off Elsie at all during the blood draw, enjoying the way she beams at him.

"All done," Cameron announces as Lily rejoins them in the room.

"The council has agreed to convene in the morning. In the meantime, both of you get some rest, and we'll talk before the meeting. I'll make sure someone is always outside your door and that no one other than Cameron or myself will enter. You will be safe so long as I am in charge of you." She smiles and squeezes Elsie's shoulder.

"We need to get word to my family that we're okay," Angelo mentions. "I'll explain to them what's going on. It shouldn't be too far if I run. I'm nervous about leaving you, though." He looks to Elsie for guidance.

"I'll be fine. Cameron, is there oxygen for Angelo to use?"

"I can get you a mask and tank, but you'll only have enough oxygen to get there and back. Don't leave it on when you get to the tunnel. I can't spare more than that."

He leaves to get Angelo the mask.

"What exactly are you going to talk to the council about tomorrow, anyway?" Angelo asks. "I'd like to report to everyone exactly why we're staying here."

"It's actually what I was going to talk about with Marjorie. I want to develop a schooling system for the children. There will be more children eventually, and they can't just work in the gardens. I have a proposal I think the council will have to acknowledge. I also want to set up a marketplace with the supplies from the surplus room. I think if we can stimulate trade, it might help remind us that we are a civilization, even if it is for a short time. But go; let everyone know we're safe. I need time to prepare this proposal if it's going to go our way."

Angelo shakes his head, amazed at her ingenuity. "That is a great idea. It will also take the burden off Mira. If people oversee specific items, it could be fun to go shopping."

He gives Elsie a lingering kiss, one that holds the promise of a bright future together. A kiss with trust and love at its core.

"I look forward to a lot more of those, you know," Elsie says, staring into his eyes as Cameron returns with the oxygen mask.

"Absolutely," Angelo answers. "I can't wait to tell everyone about your memory and what's going on. I feel truly hopeful for the first time in a long time, Elsie. Thank you."

* * *

"Well, that relationship developed quickly," Cameron comments when Angelo is gone.

Elsie tries not to analyze his tone. "It wasn't as quick as you might think. A lot of work went into it." A thought occurs to her. "He has a sister, you know. She is extremely bright and I think would be a good addition to the lab if what I present tomorrow is approved."

"Well then, I can't wait to meet her. I brought you paper and pencil so you can get your thoughts in order." Cameron sets the supplies down and sighs. "I'm sorry I took your memory, Elsie. I really thought I was saving you. Get some rest. I'm off to run tests."

Elsie sits with her thoughts. She cannot believe how much she forgot and how quickly it all returned. She's mourning her family and Max yet again but happy to have found a new community, something she never would have discovered if not for Cameron erasing her memory. She can't say things would have gone the direction they went if she knew who she was all along. Would Angelo have spent as much time with her as he did, trying to get to know her?

It doesn't really matter, does it? Now she needs to make sure their future is secure. She has a lot to think about.

She begins to write.

When Lily enters the room yet again, Elsie recalls all the long conversations she had with the actress; it's no wonder that her memories of Lily broke through.

"You had quite the adventure, didn't you?" Lily settles on the end of the bed. "By the way, how did you know about the backup supply room?"

Confused, Elsie frowns at her. "What do you mean?"

"I saw you in the supply room. We have cameras almost everywhere, you know. We have them in the garden, the prepping room, the barn, the water filtration room, and all our supply rooms. I was alerted to action in our eighty-ninth supply room, and when I went to check it out, I saw you with the others in there. I figured you knew about it and found it," Lily explains.

"Oh, I didn't know about it. We found it by accident."

Elsie recounts the events leading to the discovery, also explaining about their party and the sign-out sheet. She then decides to confide in Lily the idea that she would like to propose to the council.

"I am so amazed by all of this. I was concerned and sad to hear you had gone but happy you found these people in the cavern. They are good people, Elsie. I think your ideas are wonderful, and I'll back you up when you present them at the meeting," Lily assures her.

Something nags at Elsie. "You say there are cameras in all the rooms, including the water filtration room?" she asks, her cheeks heating.

"Yes, though they are not monitored one hundred percent of the time."

What better time will I get than this? Elsie thinks. "I need to speak to you about one of your electricians—Mike."

"I know Mike. Kind of a jerk, but he does his job. Did something happen?" Lily asks.

"Yes, I would say so."

Elsie tells Lily everything Mike did to her, as well as what he did to Hope. Lily's face clouds over with fury.

"I will make sure he is punished severely for what he has done. I will see to it myself. Thank you for telling me, Elsie. I'm honored that after everything, you would show me this trust. Now, I really think it is time for you to rest. I will wake you in the morning." Lily leaves, shutting the door behind her.

Having unburdened herself of her final weight, Elsie takes advantage of the new space in her mind and heart to organize her thoughts and write them down.

* * *

The grand meeting room is silent. Everyone sits mournfully at the tables. It has been hours since Elsie and Angelo left. All there know that if they were alive, they would be back by now.

Dinner sits untouched. Some sit with arms crossed while others play with what's on their plate. In her room, Mira is curled into a ball, crying while Marco does his awkward best to comfort her.

"What's with all the sad faces?" someone demands from the tunnel opening. Mira leaps to her feet, her pulse pounding in her ears. There's Angelo, smiling from ear to ear.

"*Angelo!*" Marjorie cries out, rushing to hug him. Mira and Marco burst from their cave and tackle him.

"How? When? How?" is all Mira can muster. Marco slaps him hard on the back and hugs him fiercely.

"Glad you're okay, brother," Marco chokes out.

"Did you find Elsie?" Marjorie asks, looking worried.

"Yes. Well, she found me, after I collapsed. I have so much to tell you all. Let's sit." He settles at the front table as the rest return to their dinner places, except for his siblings, who sit at his side, facing him. His audience listens raptly as he begins.

"So, Elsie can breathe the air." Gasps sound around the room. "*But* she hasn't been outside for five years." A few murmurs arise, and he goes on to tell them about the hospital and the doctors and scientists working there, and about Elsie and the tests they are going to conduct and what she plans to discuss with the Elite council the following day.

"They gave me an oxygen mask to wear on the way here and back."

"Back? You aren't seriously going back out there, are you? Elsie is with her people now," Amanda protests.

"We are her people, Amanda. She made that very clear to them. I'm going because I need to back her up. I won't let her face them alone."

"Now that I know there's a safe place for you to go and a safe way to get there, I'm okay with that," Mira declares. She leans over to hug her brother once more.

"I came back to let you know that we're okay. We will all be okay once we figure out how to breathe like she can, but I have to make sure she doesn't let them run tests that could kill her. They must figure it out in a safe way. I promise we will both be back when we get answers. And if we don't . . ." He looks at Mira and puts his palm to her cheek.

"Do what you need to do, Angelo. We'll be okay here," she says, trying to sound confident for her brother.

Angelo looks at Marjorie and Carlos. "Will you both be okay if I go?"

"Of course, Angelo! The more we know, the better off we will all be," Carlos says.

"Thank you. I'll see you all soon. I promise!" With that, Angelo stands and hastens back into the tunnel with the oxygen pack.

The cavern surges with life now as people mill around discussing the news. Amanda wanders up to Mira.

"He really does love her, huh?"

"Yes, he does. We should all be so lucky to meet someone who makes us feel like that."

"Well, with a building full of new people, maybe we'll have our chance." Amanda smiles and returns to her cave.

"I have no need to wait," Marco whispers slyly to his sister. "I have already declared my love and had it reciprocated."

"What? Are you kidding me?" she squeals, thrilled beyond measure.

"If you don't mind, could you watch the kids tonight? I want to spend time with Andrea."

Mira smiles. "It's about time! I will definitely watch the kids. We'll have a little sleepover. You have fun!"

Marco hugs her and runs to Andrea and the kids to share the plan. Mira smiles over at them and waves.

Things are changing, she thinks. She knew Elsie was going to bring change, but she didn't think it would happen so quickly and include so much love. Angelo and Marco have both found their forever people. The future is bright.

CHAPTER THIRTEEN

ANGELO RETURNS THAT night, to Elsie's immense relief.

"Now I can sleep with your arms around me. Don't let go."

"I won't." Angelo kisses her, something he plans to do every opportunity he has.

Lily enters the following morning, radiating excitement. "The council is ready to meet with you, Elsie my dear. We have a conference room a few floors down. Charles is a little grumpy, so expect some issues with him, but I'll try to mitigate whatever he has planned."

Elsie is determined. "Okay, let's go." She gives Angelo's hand a squeeze and gets up. "Where's Cameron? I thought he was going to join us."

"He was up most of the night working in the lab. He said he would meet us there. Hopefully he learned something," Lily says.

The three make their way through the hospital. There are at least a couple of people down every corridor, and everyone nods at them as they pass. Elsie realizes she sees no sick people.

They enter the conference room, and already seated around an oval table are seven men and four women. Lily takes her seat at the head of the table, and Charles sits to her left. A thin man with white hair and a kind face sits at the other end. They all turn toward Elsie. Charles stands.

"This is a meeting of the Council of the Alliance for Human Life and Environmental Endurance, Tucson. We are here to listen to the presentation of Elsie Fitzgerald, a member discovered during an early salvage mission and the only outsider to join the AHLEET community since its inception. She was able to survive the deadly air and radiation for months without any ill effects." He lifts his chin toward Elsie. "Elsie, when you're ready."

Elsie begins, "When I was found, I was grateful for the chance to live among you in this fine facility. However, circumstances placed me in the tunnels, where I met a group of people barely surviving. They work for you all, they eat the rations that are granted to them, and they just, well, are. There is nothing but survival giving them purpose. I then learned that even the children are made to work in the tunnels. All they know is that work. All they know is what their parents tell them, how things 'used to be.'"

Elsie pauses and glances at Angelo, who nods in support.

"What is to become of us, twenty, thirty, forty years from now, when all the people who have knowledge and information have perished? What is to become of the human race? I think it is our duty and the duty of the council to set up classrooms or a school where these children can learn. I have met a few teachers in these caverns that yearn—"

"Why speak of the future when the future is now?" Charles interrupts. "You hold the key to our survival, yet you refuse to help save civilization."

Angelo interjects, "Short of killing her and dissecting her like a rat, you have all the information you are going to get from her!"

Elsie puts a steadying hand on his arm.

Lily announces to the rest of the council, "It is Charles's wish to dissect Ms. Fitzgerald to find a cure. I want to point out the absurdity that I even have to state that this is not an option." She gives him a look of pure disgust.

"Lily, you have the least amount of education in these areas," Charles sneers. "You should not be allowed to weigh in on this matter."

"My background and money have allowed me an opinion. I also continue to value love and compassion, and *that* is why my opinions count in matters such as these, Charles!" she retorts.

"I agree with Ms. Starland," states a man to her right.

"You would, Edgar. You are both made from fantasy and fiction. I would much rather hear from one of our most educated scientists!" Charles replies.

"For goodness' sake, Charles,' states a man closer to the middle, "we all have our place on this council. I also agree with Lily and Edgar. If we start killing each other, we have lost our humanity already. It is my belief that we can biopsy Ms. Fitzgerald with her permission in a more noninvasive manner. We have been doing it for years."

"Using a laser surgical machine will drain most of the energy we save. That idea is not one we can count on," says the man seated closest to the white-haired gentleman in the front.

"We will vote on whether Ms. Fitzgerald should be biopsied," the white-haired man then states.

"There will be no vote on this manner. That is not why we came here!" Angelo yells.

"Mr. Lopez, correct?" the same man says.

"Yes, we have met many times before, Mr. King."

"I do remember you, Mr. Lopez. Elsie, I am Mr. Samuel King. I am the lead scientist on the council. I was voted such because I know exactly what our priorities are. It is not my intention to hurt you, Ms. Fitzgerald, any more than it is to kill you."

"Angelo, of course the vote is not to autopsy Elsie. It is to see if we should use the laser surgical appliance," Lily explains, though she doesn't sound convinced herself.

"It doesn't matter what the vote is! That is not why Elsie asked for the council to meet and not why we are here!"

"Mr. Lopez, Ms. Fitzgerald. It is my intention to allow you to continue with your proposal. However, I feel at this time it is important that we get this elephant out of the room. Let us vote," Mr. King says.

At that moment, Cameron rushes into the meeting, breathing heavily as if he just ran a marathon. "Pardon me, council. I must address you all. I have some extremely important information! Elsie, you said that when you were walking back from Dallas, you ate anything you could find. What did you eat?"

Elsie is thrown off balance by the randomness of the question. "Well, any fruits and vegetables that didn't go bad." She thinks back. "Oh! And there were these purple flowers—I think you called it *Astragalus*, Angelo?—that seemed to not die out as quickly as other plants. I ate the flowers, leaves, and stems. Not the best-tasting meal, but when you're hungry, you take what you can get."

Cameron presses, "Before all of this happened, what kind of vitamins or herbs did you take, and was it anything that you may presently eat as well?"

Elsie gives him a small smile. "I took regular vitamins as well as ginseng, and I made a lot of my food with ginger. I've finally gotten Angelo to eat the ginger and ginseng bars we started to make in the cavern. I told them they were great for the immune system."

"*Astragalus* is extremely helpful for asthma patients as well as for patients that have chemo. That in combination with the ginseng and ginger, I believe, are what give you your immunity. The ginseng and ginger bars might have helped Mr. Lopez last longer on the outside, but the missing component was the *Astragalus!*"

"Oh my goodness, Cameron, that is amazing!" Elsie exclaims.

"We should have enough *Astragalus* seeds to grow a crop. Then, once everyone starts ingesting this combination, we can see about living outside. It will take time, but I feel immensely confident that we can achieve this goal!"

"We did see the *Astragalus* plant in the garden. I recognized it immediately!" Elsie adds.

"We will start harvesting the seeds immediately." Mr. King smiles at Elsie, "Now that cutting you up into pieces is off the table, please continue with your plans for the children, Ms. Fitzgerald."

A bit disoriented at the new developments, Elsie takes a minute to remember where she left off.

"I have met teachers in the caverns who yearn to get back to teaching. I also believe that the children could benefit from learning from you all as well. From the workers in the gardens, the electricians, the scientists, the artists, the actors." She smiles at Lily, who is glowing with pride. "I think some of the adults could benefit from the knowledge as well.

"In addition, I would like to suggest a marketplace in the cavern, using some of the supplies from your storage. I also think employment in the labs could be opened up to people in the cavern. Let them innovate. I just think everyone in the tunnels needs more of a purpose. I think we can give them that purpose, and I think they could provide a new perspective for you folks." Elsie curtsies to signify that she's done talking and immediately feels like an idiot.

"I think it is a lovely idea, Elsie," Lily says. She looks at the others and then at Mr. King. "Well, Samuel?" The others' heads swing his way.

Mr. King straightens and clasps his hands in front of him on the table. "We will now begin the vote:

"One: the matter of Cameron searching for and creating a supplement using the *Astragalus* plants as well as collecting volunteers to test his supplement. Aye or nay?"

The room shouts, "Aye," though Charles's vote lands a half beat late.

"Two: the matter of creating schooling for the children of the tunnels and the hospital instead of having them only work in the tunnels every day? Aye or nay?"

Charles begins to protest but quails under Lily's glare. Everyone states, "Aye."

Samuel looks at Elsie. "Three: the matter of a common market to be created so that those moving about the tunnels as well as our hospital can 'shop' and the proposal to have the market run by the people from the tunnels? And that such 'shop' is supplied by our backup supplies? Aye or nay?"

All shout, "Aye!"

Mr. King continues, "It is my belief that we will need a liaison—someone to organize and set up classes and schedules, organize the market, assign responsibilities, and report to us on our progress. I nominate Ms. Elsie Fitzgerald as said liaison. Aye or nay!"

Even Charles cannot argue the idea. The entire table shouts, "Aye!"

Mr. King turns to Elsie with his gentle eyes. "Is this a role you will consider taking on, Ms. Fitzgerald? It is your idea after all."

"It will be an honor, Mr. King. I promise you will not be disappointed!" Elsie smiles.

"Meeting adjourned. Good luck, Ms. Fitzgerald. We will meet again with you in two weeks' time to see how things are moving along. Cameron, let us go to the lab so we can discuss this supplement and how to make it."

Cameron winks at Elsie and exits with Mr. King.

Angelo suddenly lifts her and spins her around. "Magnificent. You are truly magnificent," he says as he kisses her.

"I knew I would see good things from you, Elsie," Lily says as Charles grunts and lumbers past her through the door ahead of the rest of the council. "I can't wait to see what you will do next. Let me know when you come up with a schedule for the kids. Children's theater was one of my favorite activities in college. It will be fun to get back to those roots!"

"Of course! That is a fabulous idea."

"And about the Mike situation, I want you to know it was taken care of. We pulled up the feed from that day, so he has no way to dispute it. He is in isolation until he gets counseling from one of our therapists. We want to make sure nothing like that ever happens again." Lily goes to leave but turns back. "Oh, and one more thing. Before you return to the cavern, stop by the room you were in. I left a little gift for you for your party." She winks.

"Lily," Elsie says as the last of the council trickles out of the room, "I do remember that we had a very close relationship. You have been helping me from the very start; why is that?"

Lily sighs and takes a seat back at the table. Elsie and Angelo join her.

The actress studies them before speaking. "Before all this happened, I was married to a film star, Bruce Starland. Now, I wasn't a spring chicken, but I wasn't ready to be an old maid either. I wanted children so badly, and we had agreed to try after he was done filming. When the first of the bombs hit in Europe, my husband was there filming and was killed. I wasn't sure I could live without him. I went to a very dark place.

"Edgar was a dear friend who came to see me regularly. He told me that he and a few businessmen had met with some scientists, and he told me what they were up to. They knew it was the beginning of the end. He asked me if I would contribute and survive with him. Surviving was the last thing on my mind, but I agreed. Then I met with Samuel and the other scientists and doctors and began to feel it was my duty to help humanity. I knew Bruce would want me to be a part of it. Once the time came for us all to move into the caverns, we discovered others had wandered in as well. That would be your group, Angelo." She smiles.

"I saw the children, and my heart broke for them, but I was so happy that they were spared. I pushed for them to be allowed to stay and spoke to the council about having them work the caverns.

Angelo and Carlos made a compelling argument to Samuel, and I backed them without them knowing.

"Then you came along, Elsie. I saw how Charles looked at you; he saw only the answer to the future. I saw, well, *the* future. I knew you would need looking after. I felt drawn to protect you, like the daughter I never had. I watched over you on the cameras and met with you to chat. I had Cameron give me reports on what Charles asked of him and what was being done.

"When you disappeared, my heart sank. I thought we had lost you forever. Then I saw you in the supply room and felt my heart sing. I hadn't felt like that in such a long time. And when Cameron told me you returned, I knew I had to get to you before Charles did. Sorry I was a couple minutes late." She sighs peacefully. "I feel like a proud mother seeing you both together. I am sorry that you lost your family, Elsie. I hope that in addition to the family you found in the caverns, you will consider me family as well."

Elsie stands and embraces Lily.

"Of course. I would be so honored to call you family." She sees tears in the actress's eyes as they pull back.

"Don't forget to check that room. I'll see you later." Lily takes Elsie's face in her hands. "We are both so blessed." With that, she floats out of the room.

"I can't wait to go back and tell everyone what just happened. The kids are going to be so happy! I'll get right to work on how to organize the marketplace, and I—" Elsie begins.

"What situation with Mike?" Angelo interrupts. "What feed is she talking about?"

"Oh." Elsie's stomach drops. "I did keep one thing from you. The day you broke through the wall and I went to the filtration room to get water, Mike followed me and attacked me. He would have gotten pretty far if it weren't for Brian. He came in and hit him. I'm sorry I kept this from you. That's why I was acting so weird when you broke through the wall. It really messed with my head. I swore Brian to secrecy, so please don't be mad with him either," she bursts out.

"Elsie, why wouldn't you tell me this?" Angelo's face reddens and his voice rises.

"He's the head electrician, and his position is crucial to our survival. I didn't want him to retaliate. Anyway, Hope and I were going to tell you and the other leaders after the excitement died down about the room."

"What does Hope have to do with this? Why would you tell her and not me?"

"Hope was also assaulted by him." Angelo looks flabbergasted. "She asked me not to tell anyone. We didn't know all this was here and that there were more electricians and that he could be held accountable. And then Lily said there are cameras all over the caverns and in the supply room we found too. So I told her about Mike. I knew she would take care of it."

Elsie drops her gaze. "I am truly sorry I kept that from you. I wanted to protect everyone. Please forgive me."

Angelo takes Elsie into his arms and simply holds her. "There's nothing to forgive. I just wish I could have helped you through it instead of questioning why you were acting weird. I should have known better."

"You know me now. I promise I won't keep anything from you again." She holds him tighter. "Now, let's get back and tell everyone everything! I can't wait for them all to know what's going on!"

Angelo waggles an eyebrow at her. "I can't wait to get you back and continue what we did two nights ago. Do you think civilization can wait another night so I can make love to you properly?"

"I think civilization can wait another whole day," she giggles into his kiss.

CHAPTER FOURTEEN

"COME ON, ELSIE! Everyone's waiting!" Angelo calls from the opening to their cave. *Their* cave. Elsie can't believe it. Marco refused to trade his own mattress now that he has Andrea's comfort to consider, but Mira was more than happy to switch rooms with them and give them the mattress so long as they promised to keep it quiet. The fact that they now knew the situation was temporary, though, was what tilted things in the new couple's favor.

Elsie smiles at the memory of their return the day before. Once they got back, everyone was hugging them and so happy to find out about life beyond the cavern. They were even happier to learn they might one day breathe outside again. And while the kids groaned a bit at the part about starting school, there is general excitement about the marketplace idea. Now there truly is a reason to celebrate!

Angelo and Elsie spent the night and morning making up for lost time and lying in each other's arms, talking about everything Elsie remembers. Angelo then excused himself to see if any suits were left to wear to the party tonight.

Elsie doesn't need to worry about finding a dress: That was the little gift Lily left for her. The gown is a beautiful navy blue, strapless and lacy at the top and flared at the bottom, with a satin belt. Elsie can't wait to put it on and dance the night away in Angelo's arms.

She slips on the navy satin pumps Lily included with the dress. Letting her hair fall loose, she steps into the opening. When Angelo sees her, his mouth drops open.

"You look stunning, Elsie." He scans her from head to toe, then grabs her around her waist and kisses her neck. "I can't wait to take it off you later."

Elsie bats her eyelashes. "Behave. We have a celebration to get to!"

In the main cavern, everyone is dressed to the nines. The tables are set with the finest plates and flatware they could find in the supply room. A buffet table at the front is lined with carved turkey, steak, potatoes, and vegetables. There is a dessert table next to it with cookies and chips. The children tiptoe to the table to sneak cookies when they think no one is looking. Elsie notes that her and Angelo's arrival provides the thieves a perfect distraction.

"You look breathtaking, Elsie!" Mira kisses her on the cheek.

"How about you! I love that dress on you!" Elsie says as Mira spins around in a black satin cocktail dress. It flares at the waist and cuts off at the knees, accompanied by a pair of silver heels for dramatic effect. Andrea and Marco soon join the group. Andrea is wearing a peach-colored gown with sleeves that drape around the shoulders. Marco looks dashing in a black suit.

"We decided to open the wine bottles. I'll get us a glass," Marco says, kissing Andrea gallantly on the hand.

"I'll go with you. Red or white, Elsie?" Angelo murmurs into her ear.

"White, please." As the men leave on their mission, Elsie sees the other women are grinning at her. "What?"

"You are positively glowing!" Andrea laughs.

"You're one to talk! Have you and Marco made it official yet?" Elsie elbows her in the arm.

"Oh yes, they have!" Mira jumps in. "Marco asked me to watch the children while you and Angelo were away, and they made it very official!"

"Stop, Mira." Andrea peeks around as if everyone is listening. "Yes, we are official. I decided to take my own advice, and I talked to him. I told him my concerns, and he told me that he was in love with me and that nothing else mattered to him. Not our ages or our past. I had to admit that I am in love with him. Plus, the children love him too and are very happy to see us together, so that made it all the more special."

"I am so happy to hear that! Oh, and, Mira, speaking of falling in love, I have the *best* guy for you!" Elsie says, winking at her.

"Listen, I want to bask in the glory of you both and enjoy that for now! Though I will admit I am very interested in this hospital. Dr. Baker and I would benefit greatly from visiting it and seeing what that's all about! My first love is medicine, and I would love to get back to that!" Mira states as the men return with wineglasses. Marco hands Andrea and Mira a glass.

Angelo hands Elsie her wine and then takes her other hand. "Hungry, anyone? The food smells amazing! Jeremy outdid himself this time." They head toward the buffet table just as someone starts to play music through a speaker— a slow song that was popular ten years ago.

"Oh, I remember this song. It was one of my favorites," Elsie reminisces.

"Want to dance?" Without waiting for an answer, Angelo pulls her along to the open area next to the tables. They set their glasses down and begin to dance, lost in each other. He kisses her lightly.

"I can't believe all that has happened in the past couple weeks. Isn't it amazing?" Elsie says, gazing into his eyes.

Angelo moves his mouth to her ear and whispers, "I can't believe how lucky I am right now to have you in my arms after the week we just had. I promise you this is only the beginning of an amazing life together."

"Thank you for believing in me at the hospital and having my back. I never felt so protected before and more secure in anything. You make me stronger. Angelo, I love you."

"I love you so much, Elsie. I will love you for as long as I can breathe."

"Is that a joke? I don't think that's very funny." Elsie pouts, then smirks to let him know she's joking.

"Ha ha. I promise to love you forever. Is that better?"

The song ends, and they retrieve their glasses and move to the buffet table. Others who joined in the dancing remain on the dance floor for the next song.

As they serve themselves food, Amanda walks up, dressed in a red pencil dress with spaghetti straps.

"The food looks great, doesn't it?" she says to Elsie.

Elsie smiles. "Yes, it does." She then says, "I hope there are no hard feelings, Amanda. I think you are an exceptional person."

"Eh, Angelo was eligible. I knew he wasn't interested, but I couldn't stop trying." She motions with her chin as she scoops up a helping of potatoes. "Maybe the right one for me will be out there. Fingers crossed."

Elsie winks, and both smile as Amanda leaves to find a table.

"Well, that went better than I expected," Angelo admits. "I was expecting daggers since we walked in. It was a nice surprise."

"It's all been a very nice surprise," Elsie says. She turns and looks around the room. Some folks are sitting and eating the best meal they have had in five years. Some are dancing. Some are just standing around with their drinks, taking it all in. Marjorie, dressed in a sequined silver gown, and Carlos come to them with full plates.

"We were just about to sit and eat this wonderful meal. Want to join us?" Angelo offers.

"Yes, that would be lovely."

They all sit with Mira, Marco, and Andrea and eat quietly for a time, enjoying each and every bite.

Lydia appears at the table with a wide smile. "Elsie, do you have a minute?" She's wearing a pink slip dress that ends right above the knee and has straps that go over the shoulders. She looks so beautiful that it makes Elsie's heart full.

Lydia leads her over to her little cave room.

"I made this dress for the party using an old sewing machine I found in the surplus room. I started with the dress, and I just couldn't stop! There were yards and yards of material, and Marjorie said that I was the only one who was making clothes, so I should just take it, and, well," Lydia rambles, "look what I made!" Lying on her bed are a dozen shirts and pants, shorts, and blouses of different colors and patterns. Elsie can't believe her eyes.

"Oh, Lydia, these are so beautiful. You know, I think you should have a booth at the marketplace to display these and barter them. I haven't worked out the kinks yet, but you *must* be part of it!"

"Ooh, that sounds like fun!" Lydia hops giddily. "Okay, we can get back to the party. I was just so excited that I had to show you!"

"I am glad that you did."

Arm in arm, they return to the party. Lydia continues toward the dance floor.

"Lord, I hope we don't get sick after eating all this!" Marjorie exclaims back at the table.

"That is my biggest worry: that it will all come out later," Marco laughs. "I hope it's as good as it was going in!"

They all shake their heads and chuckle.

Elsie gazes out at her people. She has had quite an adventure the past five years, and it all led to this. She watches Angelo laughing and enjoying an entertaining evening with friends. Dr. Simone and Brian are on the dance floor with the children, boogying in a large circle.

There is no worry tonight. There is no need to worry about tomorrow. Tomorrow is full of new promises, new adventures, and new hope. Elsie sees a future that is bright and full of aspiration.

EPILOGUE

TODAY IS THE day the new world begins.

The main cavern has been partially converted into a marketplace, which by now consists of a number of stalls. Lydia, of course, displays her clothing. John, one of the older gentlemen, started creating stone figurines and soon had a booth of his own. People from the hospital bring snacks and other supplies to barter with. Elsie even created a small market in the hospital cafeteria for the industrial workers to take advantage of.

Everyone still works and completes their chores in the gardens and other cave rooms, but no one drags out their days anymore, trying to find something to do.

The school has taken off. Elsie enlisted Marjorie and Dominic, the other former teacher, as the main instructors, and they hold basic classes in the dining section of the cavern. The Elite invited them to the hospital conference rooms for their lessons in science, business, and of course Lily's acting classes, which are a favorite. The children are happy and thriving. They all are.

Some have moved into the hospital, like Mira, who has found her calling working with Cameron on the supplement. Once developed, they made enough that everyone could begin taking it twice daily to build up their immunity to the bad air. Long before full immunity took hold, groups began to venture out using oxygen masks, scouting out apartments and other dwellings for when it was safe to live out in the open.

From an overabundance of caution, the people of the cavern have waited about six months since the supplement's development for their lungs to tolerate the air. They have all tested the air for themselves, and they can all breathe without difficulty. Even the animals have taken well to their modified supplements. Now the time has come: moving day.

Today they will all move into the nearby town, though the cavern marketplace and gardening operations will remain where they are, and several people have elected to stay, albeit in much-improved quarters.

As they line up at the entrance, Elsie gazes down at her rounded belly — her and Angelo's little miracle. Although she doesn't know what the future holds for her little one, she knows it will be wonderful. She is due any day now, so the timing couldn't be more perfect. Angelo stands next to her with his hand on her back.

"Are you ready?" he asks softly.

"Yes. I hope you set up a good place for us while I've been busy down here," she teases.

"You and little Max are going to love it!" he says enthusiastically. Carlos opens the door, and all emerge into the world above. Though the sky is far from beautiful, a cheer goes up. Marco and Andrea come abreast of Elsie and Angelo with the children, holding hands.

"I can't wait to see our new home, Mommy!" Zander squeals, hugging his mother's leg.

"I can't wait to get my own room!" Tabby announces.

"You are all going to love the little house we found right outside town. And right next to Uncle Angelo and Aunt Elsie!" Marco says, embracing Elton.

"Anything is better than the hole we've been living in the past six years!" Andrea says firmly.

As they walk to their homes, Elsie is filled with joy. She is going home. Her new home with her new family. She moves slowly, as little Max is now leaning on her bladder.

"I hope all the plumbing has been sorted out. I have to go to the bathroom again," Elsie laughs.

"Yes, we made sure everything was in working order yesterday. The plumbers and electricians have been great in setting everyone up. All you need to do now is rest," Angelo assures her. He stays glued to her hip, his hand still on her back as if to balance her and their precious cargo.

They reach the townhomes nestled within two blocks of the town. Most of the cavern inhabitants will live here.

Marco was not kidding, Elsie thinks as they arrive at their new address. Marco, Andrea, and the children are in the home right next door to Elsie and Angelo. Elsie can't help but tear up. Their home is beautiful. All of the houses are furnished, and the new inhabitants have brought supplies from the cavern.

The supplies from room 89 haven't quite been used up yet, but they will be soon. However, Farmer David has ensured a healthy population of animals. His farm is set up just past the townhomes. Elsie promises herself she will teach little Max how to ride a horse.

"There are three bedrooms upstairs with a bathroom between two of them and of course a bathroom off the main bedroom. It is a perfect house, if I do say so myself," Angelo boasts.

"Your mother would be proud," Elsie says as she kisses his cheek. He turns to her and kisses her softly on the lips.

"I love you so much, Elsie." He guides her to the recliner in the corner. His recliner. The one they first fell in love on. "I couldn't get rid of it, so Marco helped me bring it here yesterday."

"Well, I think it is the perfect final touch." Elsie adds, "I'm going to see how Andrea and Marco's house came along."

Angelo shakes his head. "Will you never just rest?"

"*And* I have to go check on the school after that. I want to make sure the main floor is ready for the children. Try to stop me," she challenges.

This time his kiss is passionate, carrying the promise of more to come. She pulls away. "Don't you try to change my mind! I know what you're up to!"

Angelo laughs as he walks into the kitchen.

"You go. I'm going to make sure everything is in working order here. I checked it three times, but you know me."

Elsie laughs because she does know him. They both know each other inside and out. It is the most magical and wonderful feeling she has ever experienced.

Elsie heads over to Andrea's house, and Marco answers the door. Tabby shows Elsie the whole house, practically vibrating with excitement when they get to her room. The adults bask in the children's happiness. Andrea asks Elsie for tea, but Elsie declines and takes her leave.

Elsie enjoys the walk into town and to the school. Some parts of the school building have been destroyed by time, but there are four structurally sound classrooms and a main office available for everyone. Elsie enters the school to find Marjorie in the office.

"What are you doing here? You should be resting!" Marjorie scolds.

Elsie waddles over. "Why does everyone keep telling me that? I have things to do! I wanted to make sure the classrooms are ready to go for tomorrow. Is there anything we need?"

"No, everything is fine. And it is my job now to make sure of it, so let me do my job, and you go home and rest!"

At that moment, Elsie feels a warm wetness between her legs. A puddle forms beneath her.

"Oh, I've made a mess! Marjorie, I need you to get some towels and help me clean up this floor," Elsie says apologetically.

"Elsie! Your water broke! You're going to have the baby!" Marjorie shouts. She runs to the office desk and grabs the walkie-talkie.

"Brian! Brian! I need you to take Elsie to the hospital! She's having the baby!"

"What?" Elsie asks. "No, it isn't time yet, is it? I'm not ready!" She looks at Marjorie in disbelief. "Well, these things take time, right? I should be able to—"

She is interrupted by Brian galloping into the building.

"Let's not take any chances, Miss Elsie. I have the golf cart ready to go. Let's get you to the hospital!" Brian announces.

"I'll get Angelo," Marjorie says hastily, rushing out of the building. Brian guides Elsie to the golf cart.

"I still can't believe you guys got this thing to work," she says.

"Good for us that it does!"

At the hospital a few minutes later, Brian supports Elsie's elbow as they enter. One of the lab workers comes to greet them, and Brain takes his leave.

"What have we got here?"

"I need to see Dr. Baker, please. I'm having my baby now," Elsie explains. The woman grabs a wheelchair and helps Elsie ease into it.

"We'd better get you upstairs then. Should I call anyone on the intercoms?" she asks.

"Yes, please call Mira Lopez and Cameron Miller and let them know I'm here."

"Of course. I will make sure they are notified immediately."

The woman motions to her coworker at the desk, then rolls Elsie to the elevator.

When the elevator opens to the proper floor, they are greeted by Mira, whose smile is so wide it looks painful.

"I am so excited to meet my little niece or nephew! Did you want me to stay in the room with you guys or wait outside?" Mira says as she takes Elsie from the woman. "I've got her. Thank you, Becca."

Mira wheels Elsie to a large corner room. "You'll give birth here, we'll get you all cleaned up, and you will stay here for a few days until you and the baby are healthy enough to go home. Boy,

Elsie, you really know how to put a bow on things. Wasn't today supposed to be your first day in your new home?" Mira rambles at a mile a minute.

"What can I say? I'm an overachiever," Elsie says as she climbs onto the bed.

"I'll leave you this hospital gown and look for Angelo. If I know him, he is a complete wreck." Mira leaves the room.

Elsie changes into her hospital gown and ties her long hair up in a ponytail. She is so excited and nervous. *Will I be a good mom? Are we prepared to bring a person into this messy world?*

Lily enters with Cameron. "We heard someone is here about to have a baby!" she squeals.

"I don't think I'm ready for this," Elsie admits.

"A little late for that," Cameron laughs. Mira enters with Angelo in tow. He runs to Elsie and takes her hand.

"How are you feeling? Are you okay? I was so worried!" Angelo kisses Elsie's forehead and squeezes her hand. Elsie looks up to see Cameron with his arm around Mira's waist. The two started getting serious about each other a couple of months ago.

Elsie's smile disappears at the sudden, incredible pain she is experiencing.

"Oh my God!" she cries. Angelo puts his arms around her shoulders and squeezes them.

"You can do this, Elsie. I know that because you have proven so many times that you can do anything. I love you so much."

Dr. Baker enters the room.

"I hear we are going to have a baby! Okay, folks, let's give these two some privacy. It is going to be a long night." He shoos everyone out.

* * *

Nine hours later, Elsie looks into her little girl's eyes—the same deep brown as her father's.

"Hello, Max. Welcome to the world. It is a little chaotic right now, but we are fixing it. We are fixing it for you. I love you so much," Elsie whispers and kisses her cheek, imagining the day when Max can gaze up at a blue sky. She trusts that it will happen.

Angelo takes Max from Elsie and gently rocks her side to side with an amazed smile.

"Hey, little peanut. I am so happy you are here, Maxine Agnes Lopez. I know I shouldn't have cared whether you were a boy or a girl, but I did." He then sits next to Elsie on the bed with their baby girl.

Friends and family take their turns visiting, each having an opportunity to ooh and ahh over baby Max. As Mira and Marco argue with Angelo about who Max looks like the most, Elsie smiles at her family. Her heart couldn't be more complete. Taking it all in, she knows it is a memory she will hold on to forever, no matter what.

www.ingramcontent.com/pod-product-compliance
Lightning Source LLC
LaVergne TN
LVHW041936070526
838199LV00051BA/2810